The Chessboard Killer

Inspired on Actual Events

Desmond Farrelly

Prologue

Desperately banging, clawing, scraping the caged figure tried to cry out for help but inexplicably could not. Squashed into a tiny area every muscle in his body ached, each screaming to be attended to first, yet as much as he longed to alleviate some of his pain he was unable to; the area was too cramped to move freely. Besides, as sore as his body was, the searing pain emanating from his mouth was much worse. It blurred all around him, his head pounded with pain. Waves of nausea washed over him.

This hellish place in which his reality had been thrust into was not only minuet but completely obfuscated. He tried to scratch around in the dark to see if he could find a way out but it was useless; he was trapped. He felt like a burrowing mole whose progress had been retarded by four concrete walls confronting him on all sides; no matter how much he clawed and scraped it was utterly futile – he could make no headway. Instead, the cage he found himself in was made of wood not concrete but no matter how much he banged on the sides of the crate-like confinement he now inhabited it made no difference – no one ever came. Greeted only by silence and enraptured by an almost tangible sense of dread and despair, his emotions overcame him. He started to weep uncontrollably. The first time he had cried since he was a young boy.

Chapter 1

Turning the corner onto Ulitsa Novy Arbat, Joseph Darko walked the fifty or so paces until he came to the door of his apartment building. As he turned the key in the large iron gate which lead into the building of some seven stories, a faint smile appeared upon his traditionally stoic, emotionless face. He stepped inside and allowed the heavy door to swing back behind him. When he had taken a few steps inside he was greeted with the usual thunderous crash of the gates slamming behind him. He did not react, flinch or break stride.

Ignoring his mail box in the foyer; his stocky figure made its way to the stairs; other than bills and junk mail he never usually got any mail and at this moment in time he had far more important things on his mind.

Joseph started to walk up the four flights of stairs which led to his one room apartment. He never took the elevator in his building - not because of its unreliability but because he felt elevators were for lazy people and he could not abide the waiting around that was the inevitable consequence of taking it. He had no patience for such things, coupled with the idea of bumping into one of his neighbours and having to make small talk with them had solidified his stance of never taking the elevator in his building. As he made his way up the stairs, the closer he got to his apartment the more the sense of anticipation began to bubble inside him.

His heart rate began to quicken as this occasion was a little bit more special than all of the many other times before and there was a sense of achievement in his gait. The slight smile that had appeared a moment ago remained, a bead of perspiration began to form on his protruding severely furrowed brow. His sunken eyes widened as he slumped his far from sculptured body up the stairs. His nostrils began to flare a little as he reached the fourth floor, he was now oblivious to the drops of rain that were still in his style-less hair and which were, one by one, cascading down the side of his face - their progress only being stultified by the stubble on his face.

When he reached his floor, he took a quick look around to make sure none of neighbours were about. Satisfied that no one would disturb him or this perfect moment of anticipation he was feeling, he hastened his pace to the door of his apartment 4A. He lived on the floor with three neighbours whom lived in flat B, C and D. In one swift motion he turned the key, opened the door to his apartment and quickly shut it behind him.

He had made it all the way without disturbance. He took off his soaking wet coat and flung it on the floor and made straight for the window sill to the left of his bed.

The one room apartment was little bigger that a prison cell. Joseph's bed was in the right hand corner. To the left of the bed, and directly facing Joseph upon entering the room was a window sill which had a fairly uninspiring view of his neighbour's bathroom in 4C.

When Joseph reached the window sill he picked up the solitary item which inhabited the area- a bright red lip stick. His anticipation was at its greatest now. He quickly turned on his heels and made for a cabinet over the table to his left, opening it he ignored the few plates and bowls that were on the right side of the cabinet and having now placed the lipstick on the table, with two hands and a great deal of reverence and respect, he withdrew the item which took up the full space of the left hand side of the cabinet. The item normally sat leaning against the back of the cabinet in order to sufficiently fit into it. He gently placed on the table the large square piece of wood that was now some thirty years old and it showed as it was heavily damaged and chipped but was still unmistakable and could still be used for its original purpose - that of playing chess.

Joseph placed the chess board down in front of him as he began occupying the only seat in the room at the table. He removed the top off of the lip stick and carefully placed the tip of it to a square on the chess board. Punctiliously rolling the lip stick from the top left hand corner on the square he had chosen to the bottom right hand corner of the square. When he had drawn a perfectly straight line he slowly removed the lip stick point from the board and moved to the top right hand corner of the square he had originally chosen and again drew a straight diagonal line along it until the square of the chess board had been branded with a macabre x painted in red lip stick. As he leant away from the board and back in his chair he was now satisfied, the sense of achievement was strong in him, he was closer to his ultimate goal.

Looking down on the table, he could see a chess board with all but three squares tattooed with an ominous x painted in the same red lip stick. Joseph had now carried out this ritual sixty one times and was well on his way of filling all sixty four squares on his father's old chess board.

The significance of the ritual was that every time Joseph Darko killed someone he filled in a square on the chess board with a red x. Joseph had just come from Bittsa Park where he had killed his latest victim, a homeless drunk, who had the misfortune of being victim #61 for Joseph. Joseph's aim was to kill another three people so he could fill in the rest of the board with red x's. That would be his crowning glory and the idea that he was getting ever closer to that goal left him incredibly excited but for now he was spent, he moved the chess board to one side, lay his head down on the wooden table and fell into a deep sleep.

Chapter 2

Jack Wolfe awoke to the clarion call of the television in his apartment. He had fallen asleep in front of it last night whilst watching some bad Russian movie he could now not remember the name of. He had still not opened his eyes yet but the sound emanating from the TV was familiar - it was the same morning chat show that he had been woken up to for some months now.

The show discussed everything from daily events in the news, the weather, to all the latest gossip about all of Russia's, and particularly Moscow's hottest celebrities. Jack was not paying much attention to the TV but he knew that if that show was on it was after 10.00 am and as such he was again late for work.

Gradually, one by one, he opened his eyes. Blinking a few times, he proceeded to rub them gently in a vain effort to expedite the waking up process. Abruptly, he arose and sat slumped over on the couch in his apartment that he had fallen asleep on the night before.

He had a horrible taste in his

mouth and a pounding headache. He looked at his watch, it was 10.55 am. "Damn! Usmanov is gonna have my ass for lunch…"

Jack was still in the same clothes he had worn yesterday and the day before for that matter. He did a quick survey of his two roomed apartment located just off the Moscow city centre. There were empty Vodka bottles and McDonald's wrappers strewn everywhere.

Last night was like any other, he got home at around 8.30 pm after making a stop at the convenience store on the corner, purchased a bottle of the cheapest vodka in the store. He sat in front of the TV, not really paying any attention to it, and started drinking the bottle of Vodka. By the time he woke up the next day the contents of the bottle had all gone and he had a pounding headache.

Jack had been living the same routine, on and off, for some year and a half now. As he rose up off the couch, he stretched and tried to get his bearings. On TV he noticed that the local news was starting. He walked to the window, had a quick look at the world below from his third floor apartment, despite it being grey and pouring down with rain, the light still hurt his eyes and worsened his head ache. 'How am I going to face a day of work feeling like this?' he thought. 'The Bittsa Park Maniac has struck again!' said the reporter on the TV. This one sentence was more effective than any hangover cure. Jack swung around and stared at the TV, he was now fully lucid. He knew that he had to get to the precinct straight away.

Former New York Lieutenant Jack Wolfe had been working as a detective for the Moscow police force for the last year and a half. The statuesque detective of Irish American parents had been living in a self-imposed gulag[1] in Moscow since his wife had been killed just over eighteen months ago. In that period he had managed to make a living as a detective in Moscow: the understaffed and ill equipped police force of the most populace city in Europe were happy to have him. Before his wife was killed Jack's police record was

---

[1] Gulag: A collection of hellish prison camps that existed during the Soviet era in Russia which thrived under Stalin's rule, where hundreds of thousands of people were forced to work themselves to death in utterly miserable conditions.

impeccable. He got by working in Russia with the pidgin Russian he had picked up from growing up in the Russian American community in Brighton beach, New York.

For the last year and a half Jack had been working hard to drown himself in a sea of Vodka. He had nothing else to live for now and being in the self-imposed prison of Russia was not making his depression any better.

At that moment there was a loud bang on the door. 'Hey Jack, wake yourself up and let's go, there has been another killing in Bittsa Park, that sick bastard has struck again' Jack knew that it was his partner Pavel Mostovoi. He straightened his tie which he had loosened around his neck as he sat down for his first glass of many last night. It formed to the shape of his rotund belly- a belly he had acquired since being in Moscow due to his regular diet of fast food. 'If Aishling could see me now she would be shocked… and disappointed!' he thought. For a second this thought made his shoulders slump with acute depression. He physically shook himself to snap out of it, quickly turned off the TV, grabbed his trench coat and made for the door.

Chapter 3

Luke Callaghan was woken by Mathew pounding on his door. A quick look at his watch told him it was 1.30 pm, which meant he had only been in bed for six hours. The previous night he, Mathew, Rob, Will and Jean Paul had all been out at the club they went to every Thursday night – Camborio, located at the top of a hill facing the picturesque ancient Muslim settlement of La Alhambra in the Andalucían city of Granada.

"What's up dude?" Luke just about managed to spit out over his killer hangover. "Get up! we're getting wrecked!, to celebrate Jean Paul's birthday!" came Mathew's reply. Luke thought they had celebrated that last night – and pretty damn well too. "Come on man, let's go" shouted Jean Paul as he burst through the door. Luke rubbed his eyes and looked up at Jean Paul, he looked him straight in the eye just to make sure that he and Mathew were actually serious. One look at the pair of them told Luke all he needed to know.

Luke had been living with his current roommates for two and half months now since moving from living with a *madre*; a Spanish mother who cooked all his meals, cleaned his clothes and whom he stayed with for a fee paid at the start of the scholastic year. He had stayed with her during semester one of his year in Spain on an Erasmus year; a year away for students to go to a foreign country to improve their ability in a particular language. After spending four months with the *madre* he'd had enough and decided to move. He moved in with Jean Paul, from Nancy and Mathew, from Dublin at the beginning of January and right away he knew that he had made the right choice.

Luke looked out of his bedroom door which led to the living room, to see Rob and Will slouched on the living room couch which had been their bed the night before. They still lived with a *madre* but they hated staying there so they usually spent half the week in apartment 5c Calle San Anton, located right in the centre of Granada city centre in which Mathew, Jean Paul and Luke resided. Luke could see that even though Rob and Will were hurting from a hangover just as much as he was they too were in celebratory mood for Jean Paul's *anniversaire*.

Luke shouted out to the guys to

give him a minute. When he had put some trousers on and ventured into the living room he could see Jean Paul and Mathew proudly glaring at five bottles of Negrita rum as if they were their first born children. "Which one you want?" asked Jean Paul. "Where'd you guys get them man?" asked Luke. "I got them this morning at around 11 o clock, I fell asleep for like two hours and I've just been lying in bed waiting for you guys to get up ever since. I decided since we are all here today we should celebrate Jean Paul's birthday today as well as last night as today is actually his birthday" said Mathew.

"You were in danger of sleeping too much, so we had to wake you up so you could go to work" Rob said in his usual dead pan manner which made everyone in the room laugh out loud. By going to work he of course meant getting drunk. They had drank a bottle of rum each the night before and they were about to attempt the same feat again after only a few hours' sleep - even for these guys this would be an achievement. They all took their seats around the round table in the rundown apartment (the boys would not have it any other way though: if the apartment had been nicely furnished they would have to worry about the stuff which they would inevitably break during their mammoth drinking sessions), they each grabbed a bottle and a plastic cup, eye balled each other for one last time just to confirm that they were about to really proceed with a full days drinking which would only end when each of these guys had finished the bottles they had in their hands. With an air of trepidation they each twisted the top off their bottles, Will threw his bottle top across the room and the rest of the guys knew that there was no turning back. "God I am dying" announced Mathew. After very slowly pouring a rum and coke each, they raised their glasses, wished Jean Paul "*Joyeux Anniversaire*" and downed their drinks in one go. "God I feel fuckin' great" professed Mathew; the alcohol in his system from the night before gleefully welcoming the new arrival with open arms.

"Get some music going man" demanded Will which was Luke's cue to bring out his massive music collect of two 500 slot CD books which he had brought all the way from North Carolina, America. "Where the cards at man?" Rob asked to no one in particularly eager to commence the inaugural drinking games of the day.

Chapter 4

Born in 1975, Joseph Darko was the only son of Nikolai and Svetlana Darko. When he was born his mother was twenty five years old, while his father was some years older at forty two. As a family they were poor, the only income in the household was Nikolai's. He worked in an abattoir and the pay was meagre compared to the hours he had to work. Svetlana was nothing more than a poor peasant girl when Nikolai meet her. Although she was not physically attracted to him, her father was old and as he was her only family; she knew that the only way she would survive when he eventually died, would be to marry and Nikolai was her only option. He paid her father a pitiful dowry, but a lot of money nevertheless for a man who earned as little as he did. She left her father and moved in with Nikolai.

His house was located closer to the city than she was used to but they still lived in the countryside. They were soon married and not long after she fell pregnant. Nikolai was a cold person and in the early years, the best years for her, their relationship could only be regarded as cordial. When Svetlana became pregnant Nikolai withdrew all communication from Svetlana for several months. When he finally did break his self-imposed vow of silence after around five months he was a different person. Now he was filled with anger and would fly off the handle at his wife for anything she would say or do or not do for that matter. She lived constantly on tender hooks, the only time she could relax was when Nikolai was at work. She dreaded his return, during the day the more immanent it became the more agitated she would get and would often break down in tears with the thoughts of what would happen when he did eventually come home.

When Joseph was finally born, Nikolai's temper began to cool a little- towards Svetlana at least, he seemed to turn all his hatred now towards Joseph. He did not speak to his boy for the first few years of his life and did his very best to refuse to even acknowledge his existence. When Joseph would cry, Nikolai would give Svetlana a look that she could only interpret as "make that boy shut the hell up now...or I will!". She dreaded to think what method he might use, so as soon as Joseph would start to cry no matter what time of the day or night it was or what the weather was like she would race over to him, pick him up in her arms and bring him outside to calm him down as best she could before she would dare bring him back into Nikolai's Domain.

They lived in a small two roomed house, more accurately described as a shack, on the outskirts of the South eastern Russian City of Volgograd. Volgograd was formerly called Stalingrad between the period 1925 to 1961. It is sixty miles long, and is situated on the west bank of the Volga River. The city was the scene of heavy fighting during the Russian Civil War. Bolshevik forces occupied it during 1918, but were attacked by white forces. During the battle the Bolsheviks were pushed back and surrounded at first, and only the actions of Josef Dzhugashvili (later better known as Stalin – the Russian word for 'Steel'), saved the city for the Bolsheviks. In honour of Stalin's efforts in defending the city, it was renamed Stalingrad in 1925.

During Josef Stalin's rule (1922-1953), thousands of places, mostly cities, in the Soviet Union and other communist countries were named or renamed in honour of him. Most of these places had their names changed back to the original ones shortly after the 20th Congress of the Communist Party of the Soviet Union in 1956. In 1961, Stalingrad became Volgograd as part of Nikita Khrushchev's programme of de-Stalinization.

Their house was located on the South Eastern outskirts of the city, whilst Nikolai's work at the abattoir, was located on the North Eastern rim on the city. This made getting to work a real undertaking; he rose every morning at 5.00 am, caught a lift until he reached the centre of the city, then he had to get another lift with a co-worker (who lived in an apartment in the city centre) to the abattoir. On the way home he had to do the same routine, getting into the centre of town was fine but getting back home was not as easy. Sometimes he would get lucky and get a lift back home with his neighbour Alexsi, who lived half a mile up the road from Nikolai and whom he caught a lift with every morning but if his neighbour was not working late at the box manufacturing plant where he worked, as he often wasn't, then Nikolai would have to rely on the mercy of strangers - something he hated doing, and something which was very scarce during a time in

Russia when suspicion of ones neighbour was common place and even more so of strangers.

The drudgery of this daily routine did little to ameliorate Nikolai's temper or lessen his ill will towards Joseph or Sveltana. His work day was long and arduous; from the time he arrived at the Abattoir at 6.30 am he was boning beef; separating the bones from carcasses of meat. The cows were killed in one room in the abattoir, then the cow carcasses were cut up into sections with all the waste products (bowels and stomach) removed, then in the room in which Nikolai worked (and twenty other men like him, who all worked a conveyor belt line which had a constant supply of meat passing in front of them) the large pieces of cow carcass were de-boned until they had smaller pieces of meat that could be sent to a butcher shop for them to cut up into servings for customers. Other than an hour break at one o clock, this was Nikolai's day until quitting time at 7.00 pm. He sometimes only arrived back home at 10.00 pm if he had a particularly difficult time trying to get a lift in the city centre. It was times like these that a wrong word or step out of place from Svetlana or even Joseph would merit a smack in the face for Svetlana from Nikolai.

Chapter 5

Nikolai Darko, like many Russians, particularly at the time, loved chess. He regularly read copies of '64' magazine, a Russian magazine dedicated entirely to chess. If ever Joseph would try to sneak a peek at '64' Nikolai would yell at him and take the magazine away from Joseph. He longed to learn the rules and wonders of chess. Even more so he yearned to be able to share something with his father that made him happy – so they could share moments of happiness together. But deep down he knew that he and his father would never share such times.

In Russia, Chess is regarded as a noble profession. The Russian school of traditional Chess has been distinguished from other styles of play by its rigorous use of scientific methods of experimentation and systematic analysis. The best chess players were and to this day still are considered the crème de la crème of Russian Society. Chess was played by Lenin and due to state sponsorship became a sport in which Russia dominated the entire world.

The soviet system of chess was started by a colleague of Lenin's –

Nikolai Krylenko. He introduced the total dedication which became characteristic of the Soviet players who developed a style of total warfare, deliberately dragging out games or manipulating results against themselves. The Russian school encouraged the aggressive stare at the board.

Joseph eventually did learn the rules and wonders of chess, by observing his father whilst he played. Nikolai, unaware that he was being watched, would set up his chess board outside the house on the porch; wanting to be in an environment devoid of distraction, where he could truly concentrate and test his chess and in turn his problem solving skills. The house with Joseph and Svetlana was not such an environment. He would set up various challenges for himself and try to capture his imaginary opponent's queen in a certain number of moves. Whilst doing this Joseph would watch fascinated from the window inside of the house all without his father's knowledge. Nikolai thought that his son was too stupid to ever comprehend the great game.

As much as Nikolai never had a loving relationship with Joseph, for his 8th birthday he gave him a present – the first and only present he had ever given his son. Nikolai's friend Alexsi had a mongrel dog who had just given puppies around the time of Joseph's birthday and he wanted to give one of them to young Joseph. If Nikolai refused he knew that Alexsi would think that something was amiss. He did not want him to become aware of how fractured and damaged his relationship was with his wife and only child and how he mistreated them.

As such he begrudgingly gave the dog to his son for his birthday but forewarned him that the dog was solely Joseph's responsibility; that he would have to feed him and clean him, he would have nothing to do with the dog. If Joseph could not do this - then he would set the dog free in the countryside and Joseph would never see it again.

Despite his father's cruel threats Joseph was overjoyed. At least now he had a friend. He decided to name the dog Dragan. Whilst his father was at work he would play games with his new found friend all day long. Joseph and Dragan were inseparable. Joseph always went to great efforts to keep his companion away from his father because he wanted to show him that the dog was not going to be a burden to him or the family. He also knew that if his father had a bad day at work and Dragan was making noise and annoying him he may very well carry out his threat and Joseph would never see his dog again.

As feeding Dragan was Joseph's responsibility and as the family were very poor and could not afford to buy extra food to feed a dog, Joseph shared his meals with Dragan; he would give him half of all his daily meals. He was only too happy to do this for his friend and when half of Joseph's food was not enough to satisfy the appetite of his ever growing dog, as it increasingly was not, Joseph knew of a rat's nest in the woods not far from where he lived, where he would bring Dragan to ransack. This had the dual benefit of a dog that was no longer hungry and also less possibility of discovering the rodents in his house.

When Nikolai found out that his son was sharing his meals with the dog he was filled with a sense of contentment; the idea of his son having less to eat and suffering even when he was not directly punishing him brought a smile to his face. Little did Nikolai realise but Joseph was far from suffering, he had never been happier. Joseph felt having less to eat was a small price to pay for all the happy times he and Dragan shared together.

Chapter 6

One Sunday afternoon some years later, when Joseph was twelve years old and Dragan was no longer a puppy but a fully grown dog there was a knock on the door of the house. Nikolai was having a nap before dinner so Svetlana answered it. Much to her surprise it was Alexsi's wife Petra. She had walked all the way from her house to theirs so Sveltana knew that something must be wrong. Petra had a forlorn look about her and when she spoke Svetlana's fears were realised. "Alexsi is very sick, according to the doctor he will not be able to go to work all next week" Petra informed Svetlana,. She continued to tell Svetlana that Alexsi had arranged with his job that he would take his annual holidays next week, whilst he was sick, and would be sure to be back in work the following Monday. Petra told Svetlana that Alexsi was sorry but he would not be able to bring Nikolai to work all next week and that he hoped that he would be able to make alternative arrangements.

Svetlana and Petra alike knew that there was little or no possibility of making alternative arrangements and that the idea of taking holidays next week at the abattoir where Nikolai worked would be out of the question. Petra could barely look Svetlana in the eye as she reiterated Alexsi's apology and turned to walk away.

As Svetlana slowly closed the door Nikolai awoke, aware that someone had been at the door he arose in a flash, already in a rage. Blood boiling, he quizzed her as to "who was at the door?" "A man?" When she told him what had happened and who had been at the door he was unsure whether to believe her or not. 'Was she making it up?' he wondered. The troubled look in her eyes dispelled any such doubt – he knew she was telling the truth. His mind raced as to how he would get to and from work tomorrow and then the next day and the day after that. 'How would he manage all week?' he pondered.

Chapter 7

Straight after dinner Nikolai went to bed – he needed to try and get enough sleep to be sufficiently rested to face a full day's work by the time he awoke the next morning. He normally rose at 5:00 am in order be in work for 6:30 am but as Alexsi was sick and would be unable to give him a lift into the city centre this would not be an option. Once in the city centre he could grab a lift from a co-worker at the abattoir and be in time for work starting at 6:30 am.

His problem was getting to the city centre without a lift from Alexsi. It usually took them one hour in Alexsi's car. Nikolai estimated that if he left the house at 4:00 am he should get into the city on time. If he was leaving his house at 4:00 am he would have to be up at 3:30 am to eat breakfast. This meant that Svetlana had to be up at that time too. When she arose she was exhausted. She somehow managed to rustle up some breakfast for Nikolai. When he left at 4:00am she went back to bed. The thought that whilst he was making the long trek in the freezing cold morning air into town to try and get to work on time his wife and son were comfortably tucked up in bed filled Nikolai with anger. Every step he took his anger grew. His mind raced with ill will towards the two of them. Until eventually merely thinking such thoughts would no longer suffice. He began expressing his malice aloud as he walked into town on the pitch black Monday morning.

His estimation of two hours to get from his house to the city centre by foot proved grossly inaccurate – he did not arrive until 7:00 am and as such had missed any possibility of getting a lift to the abattoir with a co-worker.

He knew whenever he did manage to get into work his boss Grennady Shokhin would not want to hear about why he was arriving late, that he had been travelling for hours to get there. One thing was certain he was in big trouble as it was now 8:00 am and he was still struggling to find someone going his way.

Eventually at 10:55 am he arrived into work, he found a lift at around 10:00 am but they were only going part of the way – he had little choice but to take it. He caught a ride to the outskirts of the city, just as far as the statue of Minerva.

For the Heroism shown during World War Two, (The Great Patriotic War as it is better known in Russia due to the millions and millions of Russians who lost their lives during the war) Stalingrad was awarded the title Hero City in 1945. The Statue of Minerva is a memorial complex commemorating the battle of Stalingrad, dominated by an immense allegorical sculpture of Mother Russia, erected on the Mamayev Kurgan, a hill that saw some of the most intense fighting during the battle. A number of cities around the world especially ones that suffered particularly badly during the war established sister or twinning links with the city. Hiroshima is twinned with Volgograd.

From the statue there was still three miles to go before getting to work, he ran most of the way. When he did arrive he was already exhausted and little able for the arduous half day (at this stage) of work that lay ahead of him. As soon as he set foot onto the factory floor of his work section he was almost deafened by Shokhin's scream. "Darko! ... what the hell are you doing here!?". "I gave you the benefit of the doubt and assumed you were dead because I know even you are not stupid enough to come in late to work". Nikolai's co-workers looked up momentarily but quickly went back to work, not wanting to incur the caustic wrath of one of Shokhin's soliloquies.

As the factory sprung noisily back into life; each worker, head down not wanting to make eye contact with Nikolai in case somehow Shokhin's would deem them guilty by association. Shokhin made his way towards Nikolai. "Darko, you will work the rest of the day with no pay, you will also work through lunch!".
"Yes sir, sorry for being la…"
"I don't want to hear it Darko"
"No Sir, sorry sir" Nikolai said as he turned to get to his station to commence work. Mid turn, Shokhin said "Darko (freezing Nikolai to the spot) remember this. This is me being nice. Do not make me be mean, believe me, you would not like it". Nikolai nodded vigorously and rushed to get to work.

As Alexsi was not working he could not rely on a lift home that evening either. Nikolai had to rely on the mercy of strangers in order to get home. This was something which made him sick to his stomach but he knew he had little choice.

It was close to 10:00 pm by the time Nikolai managed to get home. He had not eaten since 3:30 am that morning. He was too hungry and tried to take out his bad day on Svetlana or Joseph. When he arrived home he ate and went straight to bed, he did not even make eye contact with either his wife or son; he stared at his food and when he had finished he rose up from the dinner table and went straight to bed. This was the cue for everyone else to go to bed too and not make a sound. Luckily, Svetlana thought to herself, no one did - not even Dragan.

Chapter 8

As he had so seriously misjudged how long it would take to make the trek from where he lived to the city centre the morning before, Nikolai knew he would not be able to afford to sleep until 3:30 am again and leave at 4:00 am. He would have to leave the house at 2:30 am; giving him little over three hours sleep to recover from the Monday he had endured. How could he manage to get into the city centre, get a lift to work, work all day and get back home again on such little sleep? He dared not think about it. The fear of Shokhin's reaction to him being late again was better than any alarm clock. At 2:00 am he shot out of bed. Svetlana had not slept all night. She had anticipated such an occurrence by Nikolai's mood the previous night. When he got up she did too, they did not speak. She just hurriedly went about preparing some breakfast for her husband.

By 2:30 am he was out the door, on his way, he did not say a word to her – he just left. She was too afraid to break the vow of silence that had implicitly been imposed upon her by Nikolai's mood.

As he briskly made his way farther from home and closer to Volgograd city centre his thoughts once again were of Svetlana and Joseph tucked up in their beds whilst he must endure the harsh morning winter wind against his face and his now numb hands and feet. Such thoughts made his blood boil. "Useless fools" he said to himself aloud. As he said it, without consciously doing so, he clenched his fists and started to grind his teeth. A minute or so later he caught himself doing it again. He instantly shook himself out of his hallucinating rage. He knew that such day dreaming about his infuriatingly useless family would only better his chances of not being on time again.

This time he arrived into the city centre by 6:05 am and managed to get a lift with a co-worker Viktor. Usually they would leave from the city centre at latest by 6:00 am. Viktor was just about to leave when Nikolai saw him and managed to secure a lift with him.

Nikolai and Viktor arrived into work at 6:35 am. Shokhin was waiting for them. Viktor was told not to allow such an occurrence happen again or his wages would be docked. Viktor looked at

Nikolai with immense hatred for making him late and promised Shokhin that it would not happen again. "Darko" Shokhin said "why do you not listen to me?"

"I'm so sorry sir…"

"You will again work all day without any pay but instead of working through your lunch you will spend it in the freezer! Maybe such a punishment will make you be early tomorrow?"

"Sorry sir", "Yes sir" Nikolai said as he turned to get to his station to commence work. "Darko you have had two chances so far with me, you will not get a third."

"No sir, sorry sir… thank you sir".

"Get to work!" Shokhin screamed in Nikolai's face almost busting his ear drums.

After an entire hour in the freezer during lunch Nikolai could not feel his hands any more. Before work recommenced again at 2:00 pm he managed to shuffle his way to the bathroom and run them under the hot tap for a few minutes. It did little to warm them up again but at least he had some feeling in them again and was able to carry on working. All day long his body ached with pain; he could barely make a differentiation between what was the dead meat of the animal carcases' he was meant to be de-boning and his own numb, lifeless hands. Throughout the day his teeth chattered and his body shivered – the cold had gotten into his bones and would not be easily dispelled.

Once more he did not arrive home till near 10:00 pm. By the second night of this gruelling ordeal he was suffering from such tiredness and hunger it left him utterly nauseous. As such he was powerless to scold his wife and son for how easy they had things in life. Again he ate in silence and went to bed directly afterwards.

As before he (along with Svetlana) arose at 2:00 am. He ate breakfast and left at 2:30 am without saying a word. As Svetlana got back into bed for a few more hours sleep before Joseph woke up, she longed for Alexsi to get better soon so that they could get back to the way things were before. He managed to arrive into the city centre by 6:00 am on the dot but Viktor was not waiting for him. Maybe he was running late? Nikolai wondered. But by 6:05 am it was painfully obvious to Nikolai that Viktor had already left for work, not wanting to again incur Shokhin's wrath for Nikolai's lateness.

Nikolai became blinded with panic, heart racing he surveyed his environs, looking for a car that might stop to give him a lift. Nothing. Everyone was doing their best to ignore him. Eventually by 6:20 am he managed to get a lift. Luckily the driver worked in a factory very close to Nikolai's abattoir but he did not have to be in work till 7:00 am.

As they drove Nikolai's mind began to race as to what would happen once he arrived into work, he wished he was already there, in work, on the boning line. He longed to just be there now doing his job without all these extra problems of getting there on time. As the car drove onwards he thought how he would gladly work through lunch again but somehow he knew that Shokhin would not be so benevolent on this occasion. His leg shook with nervous energy willing the car to move faster. The car stopped one hundred yards from Nikolai's factory at 6:50 am. Without a word of thanks to the driver he leapt from the car and sprinted towards work. He burst through the doors at 6:51 am, sweat teeming from every pore.

All his efforts were in vain though and in his heart he knew what was coming. "Darko get out!" Shokhin bellowed as soon as his saw Nikolai's sorry face. He knew that pleading his case was a futile pursuit but Nikolai was desperate.
"Please sir, please"
"You are no longer employed here Darko"
"No sir" Nikolai coughed out as his voice broke trying to hold back the emotion. This time nobody stopped working. To his co-workers Nikolai was already just a memory. As knives rhythmically separated meat from bone a truly dejected Nikolai skulked out the door of the factory where he formally worked.

Outside he wandered in a daze, barely comprehending what had just occurred. He walked stunned into the city centre, not bothering to look for a lift. From there he continued on towards home still in a daze. One step after another - with no purpose in his stride. He walked for some six hours before he reached the pathway to his home. Suddenly he awoke from his clouded state. With steely eyes fixed on his house he had one purpose – to make his family pay for their laziness, for what he had endured in the last few days, for getting him fired!

Chapter 9

Like a man possessed Nikolai pugnaciously made his way up the twenty yard pathway that lead to his house from the road. Whereas before he had aimlessly wandered for hours as he happened to make his way from his former place of employ back to his home, now his movement had a purpose. His pace quickened. His eyes unflinchingly fixed on his target destination – his house. The place where his lazy wife and good-for-nothing son where - where they had been all this time whilst he has been enduring hell over the past few days. Not once did they ask how things were going? How he was managing to get to and from work without assistance from his infirmed friend Alexsi? They did not care! he thought to himself. Almost catching himself in the acknowledgement that if they had tried to speak to him in the last few days he would have made them regret it. As soon as this thought entered his head he dismissed it. "I am going to make them pay for what they have made happen – for getting me fired" he thought to himself. Of course there was no logic to Nikolai's thought process; that somehow Svetlana and Joseph had made Nikolai get fired but to

Nikolai it made perfect sense and even if they were not directly responsible for what happened, by the very fact that they were at home enjoying themselves whilst he was having to humiliate himself by asking total strangers for lifts in order to get to work on time, whilst Shokhin was making a fool of him in front of his co-workers, they did not even know and probably wouldn't care that he had spent his entire lunch break in the meat freezer in work as punishment for being late.

Simply put, Nikolai was a bully, and like all bullies having been belittled by those more powerful than him he was now intent on taking out his anger and pain on those weaker than him, namely his family.

As he made his way closer to his house, his mind wandered, eyes glazing over at the thought of what he would do now that he had no source of income. He shook himself out of it. All of a sudden he was only ten feet away from his front porch. Dragan was playfully running towards him.

Svetlana had heard someone coming up the pathway. She was immediately concerned as no one would ever call to the house at this time during the day. When she went to the window and saw Nikolai standing outside of the house her stomach sank. Her heart began to race. If he was here, at this time, it meant something bad had happened. He looked shaken and dishevelled yet his eyes were steely. She noticed he still had his work clothes on, still had his belt of boning knives secured around his waist. Something had definitely happened. Something bad. Involuntarily she began to tremble.

Dragan and Joseph had been playing around the back of the house when they heard someone coming up the path. As they made their way to the front of the house to see what was happening, Dragan raced ahead of Joseph. Dragan made his way towards Nikolai. By the time Joseph made it around to the front of the house Dragan was leaping towards Nikolai, playfully welcoming him home. Something that he had never done before because Nikolai was never usually home at this time of day. With one blink Nikolai awoke into lucidity. Seeing Dragan in flight coming towards him. He was in no humour of 'that god dam dog' he thought to himself. In one swift and fatal motion he grabbed Dragan's neck whilst he was in mid-air with his left hand and whilst turning around took out one of his boning knives from his belt with his right hand and thrust it into Dragan's skull. By the time Nikolai had completed a half turn, he threw Dragan's now lifeless body to the ground. "No daddy, no, why? Daddy, no…please" Joseph screamed. Nikolai turned around in a flash and stared at Joseph like a rabid wolverine. Joseph had never seen his daddy like this before. Despite being scared, his love for his dog made him move forward toward his father. He wanted to see if Dragan was still alive. Nickoli rushed toward his gingerly on coming son and with all his strength gave Joseph a slap across the face with the back of his hand.

Despite loathing Joseph, Nikolai had never hit his son, he had always tried to block out his sons existence. Nikolai, a slight man of 5,6", had never hit anyone or anything as hard in his life – he had slapped Svetlana across the face before but never as hard as this. The blow sent young Joseph flying backwards a full three feet. When he hit the ground he was already unconscious.

By the time his son hit the ground

Nikolai was already making his way to the porch of the house. He did not care what state he had left his son in. He knew, or at least he was pretty sure, that he had not killed him. If he had wanted to do that he would have used his fist instead of the back of his hand to hit Joseph.

By the time Nikolai had placed one foot on the porch of his house he was confronted by a hysterical Svetlana. She had seen everything from the window. She was shocked, appalled and increasingly scared for her own life and that of her beloved son. She mustered up all her strength to confront Nikolai and demand why he was behaving like this and how he could be so monstrous?

Before she had a chance to say a word Nikolai pre-empted her. "You" he said "you lazy bitch" he lunged towards her grabbing her by the hair. Svetlana let out a yelp. Now, her over whelming emotion was fear. Fear for what he was going to do to her. The little amount of strength she had managed to muster vanished in an instant.

"You sit here all day while I break my back working" Nikolai said.

"What?" Svetlana replied. "Shut the hell up" Nikolai blasted back as he punched her in the face with his right hand, whilst still holding her by the hair with his left.

She started to wail. Allowing herself to lose herself in the pain of the impact and the horrible existence she had had to endure with such a vile man. Nikolai withdrew his left hand which had gripped Svetlans's hair and she fell to the floor, back into the house. As she hit the floor she stopped herself from crying. She knew that she would need to keep strong. Crying may just make him worse she thought. She did not know what this monster had in mind for her or what he was capable of but she feared the worst, particularly as he seemed to be blaming her for whatever had happened to him she thought. Nikolai was standing in the door way of the house. Svetlana looked up at him from the floor. The dullness of the sky behind Nikolai framed by the doorway hurt her burning eyes which ached from crying. The brightness of the dull sky was heightened by the dark surroundings inside the house.

Nikolai looked down on her with distain in his eyes. She was nothing more than a piece of dirt he thought to himself.

He slowly unbuckled his boning knife belt. When he had successfully loosened it he threw the knife belt and the knives into the kitchen sink to his left. All the while staring at Svetlana. She knew that whatever he was about to do to her would not be good. Nikolai could see in her eyes how scared she was of him. The thought pleased him. As he had been emasculated and humiliated in recent days in work in this moment, staring down at his terrified wife he began to feel like a man again. He felt good. A sly smile crept over the right side of his mouth. His eyes widened. Svetlana had never seen such a look before and was unsure as to what it was a precursor to. She had no idea what thoughts were now seemingly racing through Nikolai's sordid mind.

He walked towards her, went to the left side of her body, she was still bolted to the same position on the kitchen floor where she had fallen some moments ago. He lent over her. Running his hand along her right leg, up high, underneath her dress. Quickly he withdrew his hand from its position close to her crotch. He put his hand on the right side of her dress. On her waist and in one swift motion ripped the bottom part of her dress off. She lay there with only the top half of her dress intact and her bottom half exposed. Only her underwear covering her crotch. Nikolai went over to the kitchen sink, took one of his extremely sharp boning knives out of his belt, turned back around to her, bent down, slide the knife underneath the left hand side of her knickers at her hip bone and slowly cut up the side. Then he slowly moved the knife over to her right side and did the same. Her knickers were now merely a piece of cloth lying over her crotch, the supports which originally held them up had been cut away by Nikolai. He threw the knife off to the right hand side of the room near their bed. He thrust his right hand onto her crotch, grabbing her private parts and the remnants of her knickers and flung the knickers out the door behind him.

He stood up. She lay there, trembling and embarrassed. The silence was only broken by her sporadic involuntary whimpering. He loosened his pants, which fell down around his ankles. The pair had not been intimate in over five years. He got onto her, lying like a dead weight on top of her. She felt as if her chest was going to cave in with his weight. He proceeded to penetrate her. Each forward thrust was greeted with a cry, gasp or whimper from Svetlana, which were in turn received by a slew of venomous pejoratives from Nikolai, each more bilious than the last – castigating his wife in a flurry of hate filled invectives; about how useless and lazy she is.

Outside Joseph was starting to regain consciousness; he just about managed to get to his feet, swaying from side to side occasionally. He suddenly remembered what his dad had done to Dragan. He looked over and saw him lying there motionless. He ran over towards his beloved friend. There was blood everywhere. He placed his hand on his dog's body. It felt strange and cold. His attention was drawn from Dragan when, over his shoulder, he heard noises coming from inside the house. When he ran to the porch he was horrified at what he saw. His dad was raping his distressed mother right there on the kitchen floor in front of him. Nikolai stopping thrusting and scolding Svetlana, turned his head around and saw Joseph "get the hell out of here right now before I kill you and your slut of a mother will be next!" Svetlana cried out, Joseph's eyes bulged, his heart sank and his face reddened. He ran off into the woods.

In the background, inside the house, as he ran, he could hear his dad proceeding to rape his mother. He covered his ears and continued running. He ran until he could not run anymore. He lay down on the ground of the woods and shook uncontrollably with fear.

When Nikolai had finished with Svetlana he got up off her, buttoned up his trousers and moved towards the bed in the corner of the room. He lay down and dozed off into a deep sleep. All the while Svetlana lay there, distraught – feeling used, abused, and utterly worthless. Her body ached but her heart felt like a knife had pierced it. She felt sick. Her eyes were red and stinging from crying so much. Her throat was hoarse from screaming.

She stumbled to her feet, resting her left hand on her stomach in a vain attempt to help dissipate the throbbing pain emanating from it. She removed what was left of her clothing, put on a different dress and stumbled out the front door of the house. She could not even bring herself to look at Nikolai sleeping on their bed. One look she feared she might vomit. She knew she needed to find Joseph, to show him that she was ok.

That she was still alive at least. As she moved the sight of Dragan's carcass involuntarily made her quicken the pace of her pursuit.

Whilst Svetlana looked for Joseph, in the woods Joseph sat up. He was still shaking as he pulled his knees up into his chest. With his arms wrapped around his legs he rocked backwards and forwards whilst he replayed in his head the horrific scenes he had just witnessed. He knew he needed to go back to the house. To check how his mother was. The thought scared him. He was scared of what his dad might to do him when he saw him. As much as he was scared about the thought of going back he knew he had no choice. He could not stay in the woods forever and anyway it was starting to get dark the thought that his beloved mother might be in danger was enough to give him the courage he needed to pick himself up and start to make his way back in the direction of the house.

With every step his anxiety swelled. What would happen to him when he got back home? Would his mother be ok? Would she still be alive? Would his dad still be in such a rage? Would he be waiting to pounce on him – to give him his punishment when he arrived home? His mind raced and his fear grew. Yet his love and concern for his mother, acting like a tractor beam, brought him closer to home. When he arrived to around ten yards from his house he stopped and listened. Silence. He was unsure whether that was a good sign or a bad one. With much trepidation he proceeded closer to the house. He was welcomed by his dead friend's body lying outside the house. The blood on his body was starting to dry now, his mouth was open with his tongue hanging out. A single tear raced down Joseph's right cheek. As soon as he felt it on his skin he wiped it away. He knew this was not the time to mourn Dragan. Now he had to be strong for his mother. Without thinking, as though by reflex, he removed the knife that protruded from Dragan's skull. Once he had succeeded in doing so he wondered to himself if such an act had been out of respect for his fallen friend or to protect himself as he was imminently about to enter the house and was unsure what horrors he might encounter upon his home coming.

Chapter 10

As he got to the porch he again stopped and listened. Silence. He moved inside the house. He could see his mother's torn clothes scattered around the floor. He was somewhat heartened to see his dad was asleep and was not waiting in a rage for him to return. But he could not see his mother. He quickly scanned the room and the adjoining room but could not find her.

He went outside and ran around the house to see could he find any trace of his mother. Once he had done a full circle he was back in front of the house again. A white piece of cloth lay at his feet - his mother's underwear. He knew immediately what it was and his grip tightened on the knife in his hand. Looking through the front door into the house he could see his father lying on his back in a deep sleep. He made his way towards him, not knowing what he was going to do when he reached him. As he walked into the house his mind flashed back to his father raping his mother on the very floor where he now stood. How his dad had screamed at him – how he said he would kill him and worse kill his mother. Where was she? Had he already killed her? He noticed another knife close to the bed, the knife Nikolai had used to cut Svetlana's underwear. Joseph picked it up. With a knife in each hand twelve year old Joseph stood over his father. He held the knives over his head, pointing downwards in the direction of his dad. His jaw clenched, teeth grating, and vision blurry with tears he began to rain the knives down upon his father. Penetrating his throat and stomach initially. With the first blows his father woke up screaming with excruciating pain. Joseph redoubled his efforts. Thrusting the knives into his father again and again. Nikolai's arms and legs thrashed and flailed in the bed while Joseph proceeded in stabbing his father. Finally with all his strength he buried the knives into his father's abdomen and as he did so he stepped back in shock at the sight before his eyes. Blood everywhere, his dad struggling for life desperately trying to remove his very own knives from his stomach. Joseph fell to his knees and started to cry uncontrollably, begging for forgiveness. Eventually his father stopped trying to remove the knives from his stomach, soon after he stopped moving altogether, his breathing began to slow and within a couple of minutes he was dead.

Joseph picked himself up and moved out onto the porch, he was shell shocked at what he had just done. After a few moments of sitting there crying to himself he could hear someone calling his name. It was his mother. His heart was filled with joy. He ran towards the sound of his name, calling to her. When she heard him she too ran towards him. When Svetlana saw Joseph running towards her she stopped in her tracks. Why was her son covered in blood? Svetlana raced past Joseph and into the house, she was horrified by what she saw. "No!", she screamed, "What have you done?!" "Joseph – what have you done?" he could hear her wailing from inside the house. He was too afraid to follow his mother into the house. He just stood there rooted to the spot – crying to himself. When she emerged from the house she had tears streaming down her face. She went towards Joseph and embraced her son. "I'm sorry mama… I'm sorry". "I was afraid for you… for us". She could feel his body was shaking. He stopped speaking and they embraced in silence, crying all the while.

Svetlana told Joseph that as much as she was horrified by what he had done she could understand why he did it. She did not agree with it but knew how frightened he was by what his father had done and that life would never have been the same after what Nikolai had done that day and who was she to say he would not eventually carry out his threat to kill her and Joseph also. She agreed not to tell anyone what happened that day. They managed to move Nikolai's body out into the woods and bury him in a shallow grave. They cleared up the house, burnt the blood stained clothes and Svetlana's ripped dress, buried Dragan at the back of the house and agreed never to speak of that day or of what happened ever again.

Inside Svetlana's mind was a whirlwind of emotions, not all of them rational; she felt a mix of delight and despair, anger and anxiety, happiness and horror, the sense of freedom she felt was coupled with an equally strong sense of fear.

On the one hand she was happy that her hellish life thus far with Nikolai – a monster of a man, was over. Yet she had never known life without a dominant male figure in it; to 'protect' her and the thought of which made her quite anxious. She was delighted that Joseph would not have to grow up in a house filled with fear and hate anymore yet she was horrified that her young boy could have committed such a sadistic act, even if it was out of love for her. The thought that her son was capable of such a thing, regardless of the circumstances which preceded it, made her uneasy that he could possibly do it again. She was unsure whether she could bring him up on her own? Which of course was a ludicrous thought; as she had been bringing up Joseph on her own all his life thus far.

She was elated that Nikolai was out of her life but the way in which he had been dispatched from it made her remorseful. She did not mourn him, yet she mourned the circumstances that resulted in his death. She mourned the life they could have had together, the life that any husband and wife should have together.

She was angry that she let Nikolai treat her and her son so badly for so long, why did she allow it? Why did she not stand up to him? Be stronger? The thought of what he did to her on that kitchen floor, the last and ultimate humiliation made her blood boil to the point where the only thing she lamented was that she had not been the one to plunge those butcher knives into his stomach.

On top of all these emotions, which flashed in and out of her world like a constantly changing television screen, there was the very real fear she had about the possibility of her and Joseph getting caught by the police for what they did to Nikolai. This thought made her stomach sink. Every time she closed her eyes, all she see was Nikolai's blood soaked, shocked face. No matter how often she washed her hands she seemed never to be able to fully rid them of Nikolai blood.

Chapter 11

A few days later Svetlana and Joseph were inside the house when they heard a car coming up the drive way the sound of someone approaching, encroaching on the new world they now inhabited *sans* Nikoloi paralysed them with fear.

Svetlana ran to the window and looked out, it was Alexsi. She turned to Joseph and ordered him to go to his room and close the door.

Alexsi was coming to see Nikolai, to tell him that he was feeling much better now and that he would be able to bring him to work again next week. Svetlana explained to Alexsi that Nikolai had lost his job because he had been unable to turn up on time to work whilst Alexsi was ill. She said that Nikolai could not handle the shame of not being able to provide for his family, that he had left them because he no longer felt like a man and was ashamed of himself. She explained that two days ago she had come home from the local store with Joseph and found a note from Nikolai telling her he was leaving them and that he would send money if he ever did manage to find another job. Alexsi was

shocked. He could barely comprehend what he was hearing. He was initially surprised by his friend's actions but primarily he was overwhelmed with guilt. "If I had not been ill none of this would have happened" he said. "Don't blame yourself" said Svetlana "But how will you cope?" begged Alexsi. With everything that had happened in the last few days Svetlana had not even had time to think of such practicalities but it was true – what would they do? How would they survive now without Nikolai's income?
- "Allow me to help", Alexsi spurted out.
- "No, no it's ok, we will be ok, we will cope… somehow", her mind began to wander as to how exactly they would indeed cope.
- "What age is young Joseph these days?" Alexsi queried
- Svetlana looked at him quizzically as she replied "Twelve".
- "Em… still quite young. Maybe I can get him a day or two's work each week at the box making factory where I work? It won't be much; just cleaning up, moving stock and such things but it is better than nothing

Svetlana knew he was right and

knew that they needed all the help they could get. She agreed that if Alexsi could get Joseph a job she would let him do it. Alexsi was relieved, as he was desperate to ameliorate a situation he felt partially responsible for.

So two days a week Joseph worked in the box making factory in Volgograd city. Alexsi would pick him up and bring him home. Eventually, after several months, Svetlana found a part time job helping out in a food store in the village a couple of miles away. She only worked when Joseph worked, so when he was not working she would stay at home with him and take care of him. They managed to get by on the little income they had. Svetlana could get a small discount on food where she worked, which helped greatly.

They never spoke of that day again and after some years they did not ever think about it or Nikolai any more. They struggled to get by but they were very happy.

Chapter 12

Lieutenant Jack Wolfe was the most respected cop on the New York police force. Revered by his colleagues and feared by every hoodlum, deviant and delinquent in New York city. He had a formidable reputation for getting the job done.

In his precinct he was somewhat of a legend. The only problem was if he had to use force or somewhat dubious methods to solve a case – like run someone he was chasing off the road, not use a search warrant, shoot a known criminal in the leg to garner a confession, he would do it without batting an eyelid. Despite his impeccable ability to get results, the ambiguous nature of the methods he used drew more heat on the police force than 'the powers that be' cared for. They felt he was somewhat of a liability and that is why there was slim possibility of promotion for Jack. He did not care, he did not want to be stuck behind a desk, having to deal with a bunch of 'political bullshit' as he put it. As long as he was making the streets a safer place to be he was content.

Jack lived just outside New York

City in a three bedroom house in a middle class suburb. His colleagues at work would constantly make fun of him saying he should just go the whole hog and "move to Connecticut already". Such comments would really irk Jack because it had never been his idea to move out of the city, when they learnt they had a son on the way his wife Aishling felt it would be too dangerous a place to raise a family. From what he knew of the streets it was a point he could do little to argue against. So, much to his chagrin they moved to 'the burbs' as his colleagues referred to them.

The fact was, Jack knew Aishling was right about the city not being a healthy environment to raise a child. The fact was, as Jack would acknowledge in moments of solitude with a knowing smile on his face, Aishling was always right – not that he would admit it to her, he was too proud. In reality, even if she was not right, Jack would do what she wanted just to make her happy because even if she worried - sometimes a little too much – it was only out of love for Jack and their only son that she did.

They met when Jack was a rookie cop and Aishling was in her final year of an International Languages and Arts Degree in New York University (N.Y.U.). A mutual friend introduced the two of them on a night out; Jack was out with some other cops from his graduating class who had been placed in various precincts around the city and Aishling was out with some of her class mates from college.

As soon as they met that night, all those years ago, in a dingy Irish bar - that has long since been replaced by some trendy coffee shop – they were totally enamoured with each other. They spent the night lost in each other's eyes, deep in conversation. Despite being there with other people they spent the whole night together in a booth at the back of the bar near the toilets. Every so often a member of one of their respective parties would venture over to pester them to come spend some time with them. One by one they soon realised the futility of doing so; despite their friends best efforts Jack and Aishling remained transfixed by one another all night.

They soon were sharing an apartment together and after a year; just as Aishling was finishing the final semester of her degree she fell pregnant.

Nine months later they had a son and they were blissfully happy but they soon realised that the apartment they were living in would not be sufficient for a growing boy and that the city was no place to raise a family.

They moved to the suburbs to a house with a front and back garden – a place for their little boy to play as he was growing up. Jack and Aishling got married soon after their son first birthday. It took some time to save enough money for it but Jack wanted to give Aishling the wedding of her dreams. In Gaelic Aishling means 'dream' and Jack used to always say to her when he was saving for their wedding that she was the woman of his dreams and he wanted to fulfil hers by having a magical wedding for her.

In truth it was far from magical but she did wear the dress she had always imagined wearing on her big day. They were married in their local parish church, by the local Catholic priest - Fr. Shane Clancy. All their friends and family were there. For a one income, young family in their mid to late twenties it was all they would have hoped for and as far as Aishling was concerned the fact the she was married to a great man like Jack was all she cared about.

Chapter 13

As the years went on, the house Joseph and his mother now shared was filled with love and laughter. Whereas before the house was filled with tension; fear of saying the wrong thing, fear of putting Nikolai in a bad mood, fear of incurring his wrath. They would laugh about the silliest things just because now they were in an environment where they were free to do so. Joseph would often try to teach his mother how to play chess. He would set up games between himself and his mother on his father's old chess board. Such games would never last long as Svetlana would get bored and deliberately lose. Joseph knew as much but didn't ever mind, he just wanted to be spending time with his mother and having fun with her.

A freak accident around the time of Joseph's 19th birthday was to abruptly end his fledgling utopian existence in the countryside, on the outskirts of Volgograd, with his beloved mother Svetlana. This incident would be a pivotal point in Joseph's life and would be the tipping point of his tragic decent into insanity – the seeds of which had been sown in his early childhood with his father's treatment of him and exacerbated by the act of killing of his father. Yet it had quelled in the years which followed that event as he had been truly happy living with his mother. That Spring day would leave Joseph so scarred that he would seek to punish all who had the misfortune to cross his path thereafter.

That day Joseph was at the back of the house chopping wood. Svetlana took some of the wood that he had just chopped into the house to put on the stove. She was meant to come back out to collect some more so Joseph continued chopping whilst his mother went into the house. Whilst bending down to put the wood into the stove Svetlana slipped on the grate in front of it, banged her head against the stove as she fell to the ground and died instantly. Her motionless body lay flat on its back, her now lifeless eyes starring ceaselessly at the ceiling about her.

After some time, when his mother has failed to return to collect the rest of the wood he had chopped, Joseph decided to bring some in to her himself. When he got to the front door and saw his mother's body on the ground, feet pointing skywards, soles facing him, the wood he was carrying tumbled to the ground.

He rushed over to her, calling her, shaking her; hoping that she would spring into life again and break free from this paralytic state which had empoisoned her, leaving her motionless.

The tragic realisation that she, his dear mother, was dead was too much for Joseph to cope with. In a rage, he started to thrash the house, but soon realised how futile such an endeavour was. He lay down beside his mother in the foetal position, placed one arm across her and wept uncontrollable. After some time he became exhausted and fell into a deep sleep beside his now dead mother.

When he awoke several hours later the Joseph of old was gone. He got up and surveyed the now thrashed shack that was once his home. With dark ominous eyes, brow furrowed he picked up his mother, brought her outside and buried her at the back of the house beside where Dragan had been buried seven years earlier.

He came back into the house and set it on fire, but not before picking up his dead mother lip stick – lip stick he had given her for her birthday some years back with money he managed to save from working at the box factory with Andrei. When she wore it, she was luminous; she had never worn such things in her life before and by doing so made her feel like a lady for the first time in her life. He put it in his pocket, he also grabbed his father chess board and walked out of the burning house towards the road – he refused to look back – that life was dead to him now and he would make the world pay for the childhood he had, for his monster of a father, for the psychologically deleterious way he treated him his whole life and for allowing his mother to die as she did so young. He would obtain his retribution on whomever he saw fit.

Chapter 14

He walked for around forty minutes toward Volgograd city centre before he saw a car. When he did he tried to grab a lift but the driver ignored him – this only intensified Joseph's anger. Thirty minutes later someone did stop and offered Joseph a lift.
- "Where you going son?"
- "Volgograd city centre".
- "Ok, hop in, I'm not going that far but I can get you to the outskirts of the city".

      Joseph got into the mid-sized pickup truck and they set off. "I'm Sergei by the way" to which there was no response. Joseph merely ignored the driver disinterestedly and stared out the window of the truck. "Got a name son?" Sergei queried. Joseph swung his head round and stared into Sergei's eyes in a manner that startled the driver. "Yes" was Joseph's only reply. "Well, what is it then?" Sergei said with a nervous smile trying to dissipate the tension that had just shrouded them in the truck as they moved along. Joseph simply turned and looked out the window again, ignoring Sergei. After what felt like an eternity of silence to Sergei; he hated silence, he decided to try and instigate a conversation again with Joseph. This time he opted for a different tact. He noticed the chess board Joseph had with him. "Why you carrying around a chess board?" he asked. To which he received no response. "You like chess do you?" Sergei forayed one last time.

Joseph swung around and stared at Sergei again. The look in his passenger's eyes made Sergei instantly regret ever saying anything now. Joseph proceeded to tell Sergei about the chess board and its significance; how it was his father's, how he would never let him play chess, how he thought he was too stupid to play the great game, (Sergei stared at Joseph stunned at what he was hearing) how he had killed his father (Sergei heart sank) and how he was going to kill him now too.

Before Sergei could even begin to come to terms with what was happening Joseph picked up the chess board that had been on his lap, held it with a hand on either corner of the board and smashed one of the pointed edges of the chessboard into Sergei's temple. Smashing down blow after blow onto his helpless victim's head he soon killed him. Joseph took control of the wheel and brought the truck to a stop. When he looked over at Sergei, he saw that he had succeeded in smashing a hole into his head with the chess board. The sight of his victims open skull amused Joseph. He opened the driver's door and threw the body into the deserted street. He got into the driver's seat and gently placed the board on the passenger seat. He started up the pickup truck, reversed and drove over Sergei's dead body which lay in the middle of the road. As he started off on his journey in Sergei's truck, he rolled over Sergei's cadaver one more time for good measure.

Joseph bypassed Volgograd city and was back in the countryside again as he drove northwards. Whilst driving he knocked down a hitch hiker that stood at the side of the road just for the fun of it. Another, he picked up and later forced to get out; told her that she would have to run for her life. He chased behind her for miles until he eventually got bored of toying with her, sped up and ran her over, killing her.

As he drove onward into the night towards the beating heart of Russia that is Moscow, a maniacal malevolence glittered like shimmering flecks of gold leaf in the neophyte serial killers steely eyes, which were fixed steadfastly on the road in front of him. An unerring grin seemed permanently etched on his face, wells of saliva started to form at the edges of his month. He felt alive, he felt like he was ascending to his rightful status as a supreme being; to his rightful hegemonic position amongst other people, better that all other humans – he felt like a god.

Chapter 15

When Joseph arrived in Moscow, the chess board which lay on the passenger seat of Sergei's van had acquired some strange markings on it; four squares had been tattooed with lipstick, his late mother's lipstick. Each of the four squares had an x covering it. The first square represented the killing of his father seven years ago.

The first thing he noticed when he arrived in Moscow was the number of people; he had never seen so many people before in his life. The second thing he noticed was the sheer size of the city along with its majestic monuments. The third thing that caught his attention was the hysteria that had enraptured the city concerning someone the newspapers referred to as 'The Rostov Ripper'.

Joseph settled in an area of Moscow called Novy Arbat, east of the centre city; an area full of high rise, low rent, rundown apartment buildings. He managed to find a job in a supermarket located not far away from where he lived stacking shelves. Although he did not make much money he was happy with his new life; he managed to adapt to the strange and wondrous city relatively quickly despite its stark contrast to where and how he had spent all of his life up to that point.

Despite his contentment at his new way of life and despite having to try to cope with the recent tragic loss of his beloved mother neither did much to quell his new found lust for killing.

As time went on he began to learn more about the Rostov Ripper, the more he learnt the more fascinated he became with the man who had acquired the *surnom* Vitali Chikalito. Chikatilo had been a teacher and a member of the Communist Party, but as he grew older he began stalking children, disembowelling and mutilating them. His crimes were overlooked for so long partly because he was a Communist Party member and partly because the Russian weren't keen to admit a child killing sadist was stalking their utopia. This may explain why serial killers were so prevalent in Russia during this period and have been ever since.

Chikatilo was born in 1936. His childhood was quite traumatic, particularly as the USSR was soon at war with Germany and Stalin's plans of agricultural collectivisation had recently caused a famine. During the Great Patriotic war, Chikatilo witnessed some of the effects of German bombing raids. With his father at war, the young Chikatilo had to share a bed with his mother. He frequently wet the bed, for which his mother beat and humiliated him.

Chikatilo did well at school, but failed his entrance exam for Moscow State University. After finishing national service in 1960, he started to work as a telephone engineer. Chikatilo's only sexual experience in adolescence was when he, aged 18, jumped on a 13-year-old girl (his sister's friend) and wrestled her to the ground, ejaculating as the girl struggled in his grasp.

He married in 1963 a woman that his younger sister introduced him to. The couple had a son and daughter. Chikatilo later claimed that his marital sex life was minimal and that he would ejaculate on his wife and push the semen inside her with his fingers. In 1971, he completed a degree in Russian literature by a correspondence course and tried a career as a teacher. There were several complaints of him perpetrating sexual abuse on his students that were usually handled quietly and without police involvement, thus he was able to move from school to school.

In 1978, Chikatilo moved to a small coal mining town near Rostov-on-Don, where he committed his first documented murder. On December 22, he lured a nine-year-old girl to an old house and attempted to rape her. When the girl struggled, he stabbed her to death. He ejaculated in the process of knifing the child; from then on Chikatilo was only able to achieve sexual arousal and orgasm through stabbing and slashing women and children to death. Despite evidence linking Chikatilo to the girl's death, a young man, Alexsandr Kravchenko, was arrested, tried and executed for the crime.

He did not murder again until 1982, but in that year he killed several times. Chikatilo established a pattern of approaching runaways and young vagrants at bus or railway stations, enticing them to a nearby forest, and killing them. His victims were all women and children. The adult females were often prostitutes or homeless women who could be lured with promises of alcohol or money. Chikatilo would typically attempt intercourse with his adult female victims, but he would usually be unable to get an erection, which would send him into a murderous fury particularly if the woman mocked his inability to perform. He would achieve orgasm only when he stabbed the victim to death. His child victims were of both sexes; Chikatilo would lure them to secluded areas by promising them toys or candy.

On November 20, 1990, Chikatilo left his house with a one gallon flask of beer. He wandered around the city with the flask. The fact that Chikalito kept approaching children triggered the decision by the police force to arrest him.

Upon arrest, the police uncovered another piece of evidence against Chikatilo. One of his latest victims had been a physically strong (although mentally challenged) sixteen year old boy. At the crime scene, the police had found numerous signs of physical struggle between the victim and his murderer. One of Chikatilo's fingers had a relatively fresh wound. Medical examiners concluded the wound was from a human bite. In fact, his finger bone was broken. Chikatilo never sought medical attention for the wound.

The strategy chosen by the police force to make him confess was somewhat unusual for the police at the time. One of the chief interrogators kept telling Chikatilo that they all believed he was a very sick man and needed medical help. This gave Chikatilo hope that if he confessed, he wouldn't be prosecuted by reason of insanity. Finally a psychiatrist was invited to help Chikatilo (involvement of a psychiatrist during investigation was something the police had never done before). The psychiatrist was very sympathetic to Chikatilo's mental problems. After a very long conversation, Chikatilo confessed to the murders. Again, confession was not enough to prosecute him. Interrogators still needed hard evidence. Chikatilo volunteered to provide evidence – he spoke of buried bodies that the police hadn't discovered yet. That was it: the police had enough evidence to put him on trial. Chikatilo confessed to and described fifty six murders. Three of the victims had been buried and could not be found or identified, so Chikatilo was not charged with these crimes. The number of crimes Chikatilo confessed to shocked the police, who had listed only thirty six killings in their investigation. A number of victims had not been linked to the others because they were murdered far from Chikatilo's other hunting grounds, while others were not linked because they were buried and not found until Chikatilo led the police to their shallow graves.

When sentenced he was found guilty of fifty two of the fifty three murders and sentenced to death for each offence. When given a chance to speak, Chikatilo delivered a rambling speech, blaming the regime, certain political leaders, his impotence (even removing his trousers at one point) and defending himself by pointing to his childhood experienced in the notorious famine which took place in Ukraine in the 1930's.

When he stood trial the entire city, the entire country was gripped with suspense at what would be the outcome. Chikatilo's trial in 1994, full of descriptions of how he'd boiled and ate testicles and nipples, was the first celebrity serial killer trail in the former USSR. He was killed by firing squad in 1994.

By the time of Chikalito's death, Joseph Darko had become utterly enthralled by the man and the magnitude of murders he had committed. He began to become obsessed with emulating Chikalito's feats, he became fixated upon outdoing them; possessed by the idea of becoming Russia most notorious serial killer himself.

He started off by killing homeless drunks. He chose a relatively quiet park on the outskirts of the city centre called Bittsa Park. The park was located in a run-down area of Moscow.

Bittsa Park is the last metro stop on the orange line of the Moscow Metro. It is located several miles in a South Westerly direction from red square. One of Joseph's colleagues at work lived in the area and had complained of the number of homeless drunks that frequented the park. Upon hearing this Joseph knew that these people would make easy prey and would get him on his way to achieving his goal of killing more people than Chikalito.

He would befriend a lone drunk in the park; offer them some vodka he had stolen from the supermarket where he worked. His offer was a welcome change for the homeless drunks who were used to far cheaper and more potent concoctions.

Vodka usually has an alcohol content of 35% to 50% by volume. The classic Russian vodka is 40%. Dmitri Mendeleev in 1894 found that the perfect percentage for Vodka was 38%. However since spirits in his time were taxed on their strength, the percentage was rounded up to 40 to simplify the tax computation. Above this strength Vodka can burn. There is much debate as to the origins of the word Vodka, many connote the word with the Slavic word "Voda" meaning "water" – other feel that its origins lie in the name of the medieval alcoholic beverage aqua vitae (Latin for "water of life").

Amongst the very poor and homeless in Russia, black market vodka or "bathtub" vodka is widespread, as it can be produced easily to avoid taxation. However, severe poisoning, blindness, or death can occur as a result of impurities. Industrial disinfectants have been found to be present in the drink.

Once Joseph had gained their trust and gotten them sufficiently ossified he would smash their heads in with the very bottle of vodka they had been drinking from or with a large rock, until he had killed them. Every killing would merit a new x on the chess board. The enjoyment and rush he first gleaned from killing quickly began to turn into dependence; he began to crave killing people, need to kill people in order to live himself.

Chapter 16

One day at work near the end of his shift, Joseph was throwing empty boxes of soup cans, which he had just been stacking on the supermarket shelves, in the bins round the back of the supermarket when he noticed a stray dog looking for scraps of food. Although the scavenging mutt looked nothing like his childhood friend Dragan, somehow he reminded Joseph of him. It wasn't long before Joseph started to steal a little food from the store every day and when he would put the rubbish out at the end of his shift in the evening, he would give whatever food he had managed to steal to his new friend who would be expectantly waiting for Joseph by the bins. It became so that the highlight of Joseph's day would be to put the rubbish out in the evening because that would be when he would see his new friend. The dog reminded Joseph so much of his childhood friend that he began to even call him Dragan too – the stray mongrel even seemed to like being called by a name Joseph thought.

For months these evening rendezvous' took place and Joseph was as blissfully happy with this new dog as he was as a boy in Volgograd in his childhood dog. His lust for murder even began to subside during this time.

All this came to an abrupt end when Joseph's boss at the supermarket Mr Gudhov, began to become suspicious of Joseph spending such a long time every evening putting out the rubbish and also how increasingly small amounts of stock was continuously going missing throughout the store. Mr Gudhov's suspicions of Joseph were well founded and when he discovered what was actually happening he was furious.

One day when Joseph's shift was coming to an end he, like every other day, went out to the bins around the back of the supermarket to see Dragan. When he got there he was shocked to see that there was no Dragan.

Unbeknownst to him, his boss Mr Gudhov, had followed him outside and was standing behind him. "Darko!" Mr Gudhov yelled from his position of mere feet behind where Joseph was standing at the bins. Startled - Joseph swung around. "Mr Gudhov" Joseph began, but before he could even start to explain what he was doing or who he had been looking

for Mr Gudhov interrupted him.
- "You steal from me to give to some flea infested stray dog and think you will get away with it? Who do you think you are dealing with Darko? Do you think I am a fool Darko? Do you?" Mr Gudhov said as he moved right into Joseph's face increasing the volume of his rant with every step.
-"No sir, I don'"
- "Save it you ungrateful worm – you're fired!"

Mr Gudhov went to go back into the supermarket but after a few paces he turned to see Joseph glued to the same spot – stunned to be newly unemployed, stunned that Mr Gudhov had found out what he had been doing.

- "Oh and Darko, if you are looking for that mangy dog… try looking in that bin in front of you!" With that he re-entered the side door of the supermarket and slammed it shut behind him".

Joseph was unsure whether to believe Mr Gudhov or not, his hand was shaking as he opened the lid of the bin to his side with his left hand. After tentatively creeping it open a few centimetres in one motion he swung it open. Lying there on a pile of rubbish, tongue hanging out of his mouth like his childhood dog was after he had been slain by his father outside of his house was his new friend. Dead. Mr Gudhov had killed him as a penance for all the free food he had stolen from him. This was his way of taking retribution.

As much as Joseph was shocked and upset his mind quickly moved to how he would exact revenge. "You will regret that, fat man, believe me you will pay for that!" he said under his breath as he picked Dragan's body out of the bin and walked away from his former place of employ with his fallen friend in his arms.

Chapter 17

On May 26th 2006 Jack and Aishling celebrated eighteen years of marriage together. Their son was getting ready to go off to college to study the same course his mother had taken in the same college she had attended. Aishling had become a lecturer of Arts and Languages in N.Y.U. so there was a distinct possibility that he would have his mother for one of the classes he was taking – a prospect he was not looking forward to despite how much he loved her. If his new class mates were to find out, and it would not take long for them to, he would be really embarrassed.

Even though Jack and Aishling were together almost twenty years and were now in their forties they still found each other as attractive as they did that fateful night all those years ago when they were first introduced in O'Donoghue's Bar.

6,3" Jack was in great shape for his age. His body was no longer as sculptured as it was when they first meet; he no longer had toned abs but he was lean and fit particularly for a man of his age.

When they met Aishling, 5,5 and ¼" (the ¼ was very important – at least to her) had a very athletic body but now in her mid-forties she had a less svelte look about her but Jack preferred it that way; with a 'little more meat of her bones' as he put it. They both made an effort to run a few kilometres a week and that kept them healthy and looking and feeling young.

    Jack was ruggedly handsome; he had chiselled features, was seldom clean shaven and had a scar over his left eye. Aishling had always had perfect skin as long as Jack had known her, a button nose and perfectly rounded cheeks, which only became more accentuated when she smiled. When she did, Jack would jokingly say she looked like a chipmunk. She would always feign annoyance, whenever he would say this to her, but secretly she liked it when he playfully called her that. She had always, or at least as long as Jack had known her, had shoulder length chestnut coloured hair that would sometimes cascaded over her eyes. She loved it when he would still pull her close, with one finger move the hair that was obscuring her vision to one side and embrace her. She could stay there for hours she often thought to herself- resting her head on his chest wrapped in his strong arms. They were like two pieces of a jigsaw they would jokingly say to each other – a perfect fit; destined to be together forever.

Chapter 18

In the summer of 2007, New York City was being terrorised by a psychotic serial killer known only as 'Big Foot'. He had already killed eight people. Jack was head of the task force in charge of catching the city's biggest scourge. He had acquired the name from an amalgamation of vague eye witness accounts of an abnormally large figure spotted lurching away from the crime scenes.

Jack's team had managed to create a profile of 'Big Foot'. He was over 6,6" tall, white, late thirties, he had a limp in his right foot. He wore big black army boots- only ever half way laced up. An oversized all weather kaki army jacket with the hood always pulled half way down over his face.

He carried an old silver Donnay tennis racket bag over his right shoulder. But instead of a tennis racket inside there was the weapon he used to massacre his victims with – a fireman's axe. Jack had checked out the possibility that some disenfranchised ex-fireman was terrorising the city but nothing checked out.

In reality 'Big Foot' was just

someone who hated the world and everything in it. One by one he wanted to hack the face off every person in it. There was no rationale behind what he did, no particular reason. He could not handle modern life, he had become embittered by living in the 'dog eat dog' world that was New York City. He had vowed to become the scariest dog out there and kill anyone and everyone that got in his way- even those who unintentionally did so.

He particularly hated women and so far six out of his eight victims had been female. With the men he had killed he simple hacked away at them indiscriminately until they died but with his female victims he was more clinical; he would take a memento from them to remember them by, a finger, a hand, a foot, a nipple, an ear.

Jack had become obsessed with the case; it was all he spoke about and Aishling often hoped that they would catch him soon so she could get her old Jack back.

'Big Foot's' latest victim, his ninth, had been discovered in Central Park underneath a walk bridge by a couple of teenagers who had been looking for a secluded place to make out. When Jack arrived on the scene it was dark, around 10:30 pm and pouring with rain. The teenagers were pretty shaken by what they had seen and Jack instructed one of his men to drive them home, as they would question them tomorrow. He walked under the bridge, the body was lying face down, torso naked, only wearing a pin stripe blue skirt. There was no signs of sexual interference- there never was with 'Big Foot' he thought to himself – but he had continued his pattern of taking a souvenir from his female victims. This time he took his young victims, a pretty and petite girl, fingers and toes. "Jesus Christ" Jack said aloud. Two members of the forensics team, one lining out the body and the other taking photographs of the crime scene and of the victim stopped momentarily. Jack had seen enough, he turned around and made his way to his car. It was late and there was nothing much he could do at this time of night. He knew he would have to wait for the forensics report in the morning and his teams report regarding what people in the area had seen – if anything, before he could do anything. He would get an early start on it in the morning.

Waiting for Jack at his car were a band of reporters who had been tipped off that 'Big Foot' had struck again. As he approached they switched on their TV cameras, shoved them in his face and began a blitzkrieg of questions. "Lieutenant Wolfe, are you beginning to worry that you may never catch this 'Big Foot' guy? "Lieutenant Wolfe, 'Big Foot' is terrorising the city, what are you going to do about it?" "How many more victims will there be before you manage to catch him?"

When he had made his way past them all and managed to open the door to his car he turned and looked directly into the rolling camera of Channel 9 news and said –
"I am going to catch you, you sick asshole, you are nothing special, just another psychotic maniac – no more, no less. You are probably some kind of closet transsexual, who hates himself for it and that's why you target women. You hate women because there is a part of you that wishing you were one!"

The reporters and cameramen were aghast for a moment at what Jack had just said, had they heard right? They knew he had an unusual style but this was something else. As he drove off he thought to himself there was probably not an ounce of truth in what he had just said but that he may just piss 'Big Foot' off enough to make him sloppy to the point where he might make a mistake and then he would catch him.

As he drove up the driveway to his house he could see Aishling was waiting for him standing in the doorway. He could see she was annoyed.
-"Your comments are all over the news", she barked as he walked towards her upon exiting the car.
-"Good", he said, "hopefully that will piss him off enough to make his get sloppy cause right now we have nothing". He was standing in front of her now as he stood guard at the doorway of their home.
-"I hope you know what you are doing" she said as she fell into his arms. He did not reply but thought to himself that he hoped so too.

Jack's strategy did manage to work, he did piss 'Big Foot' off enough with his remarks to goad him into making mistakes, to make him become sloppy enough that they could catch him. The problem was he had miscalculated just how much his comments would effect

'Big Foot' and what his next move would be.

'Big Foot', like most other people in New York City had seen Jack's comments. When he did he was furious. He wanted to cut his heart out with his axe. He was in the process of plotting exactly how he would do it and where when he stopped himself. "Wait a minute" he said aloud to himself in his dingy empty New York apartment "Wait a god dam minute" he continues as he paced around his kitchen come living room in his one bedroom apartment. He stopped and stared at his bloody axe which was lying on the table to his right, drenched in blood from his latest victim whom he had slaughtered only hours ago in Central Park. "I'll cut his heart out alright, when I have finished with that pig he will wish I had just killed him. He has made a personal enemy of me now and I am going to make him regret it."

Chapter 19

'**The Bittsa Park Maniac has struck again'** read the headline of the front page of Tvio Dyen (Your Day) the daily Russian tabloid newspaper. The story had fascinated reporter Yevgani Stankovic ever since the police had managed to piece together various embers of evidence to discover a pattern to the killings that had been taking place in the park in the previous eight months. Up to this point the maniac was responsible for some eleven killings.

Yevgani's editor rejoiced at his ability to capture the sheer gruesomeness of each fatality; keeping readers breathless as they read. "Police have announced that there is another one dead, Stankovic!" his editor announced as he cheerily waddled into the office kitchen. Yevgani lifted his head from his computer monitor to see nobody in front of him. He was just about to re-busy himself with what he was doing when the culprit of the original interruption emerged from the kitchen carrying a full pot of coffee all for himself "I feel another good sale tomorrow" he announced to himself and to no one in particular in the crowded news room as he disappeared back into his office closing the door behind him. Yevgani knew that this was his cue to stop whatever story he was working on and get busy covering this breaking news.

Bittsa Park is a vast public park in the South West of Moscow city centre. It is nothing like Gorky Park which was heavily populated with tourists. Bittsa park is thick with forestation, with narrow pathways scarred into it to create make shift walk ways. These walk ways were strewn with litter and cigarette butts and whilst Gorky Park is a favourite with tourists, Bittsa Park was more likely to be frequented by homeless drunks and prostitutes.

Thirty five year old Yevgani Stankovic, a slight man who stood no taller than 5'7" dressed like he had just be teleported from 1978; he had ruffled hair that covered his ears, a goatee, half glasses that rested mid-way down his nose. He wore large open collar shirts with bell bottoms and Cuban heeled shoes and was never seen without a paisley neckerchief. He had a wickedly macabre way of describing the Bittsa Park and its environs; he made it seem almost haunted, as if it was located in some cursed place akin to Bram Stokers' Transylvania and not on Muscovites doorsteps, which it actually was.

It seemed to Yevgani's editor and to all the readers of Tvoi Dyen that he had managed to gain an almost unique insight into the killings that were taking place in the park. He had the ability to transport readers to the crime scene, to the point where they felt they were actually reading an eye witness account of the murders.

The police were beginning to speculate whether the victims were being felled by an escaped mental patient from a psychiatric hospital which lay at the heart of the park. The chief nurse of the hospital had conceded that sometimes patients deemed not to be dangerous were allowed to go out on walks around the park and on occasion they never came back. It had also been noted that patients classed as dangerous had escaped the hospital over the past year and had never been found.

The latest victim, a homeless drunk, had his head smashed in with a Vodka bottle but what made this victim slightly different from the others was that the Vodka bottle had been gruesomely plunged into the victims head, so that when he was found he still had the bottle protruding from the side of his head - the killer was becoming increasingly cocky, Yevgani thought, and beginning to demonstrate a temerity towards increasingly quixotic methods of killing his victims.

Chapter 20

For a few days after Jack's remarks there were no 'Big Foot' related incidents. Naively some of Jack's less experienced colleagues thought that maybe his comments had managed to scare him into stopping. Jack knew better, he knew that sick bastards like 'Big Foot' would not stop so easily. The only way to stop them was to put them in jail and throw away the key or kill them. He did not care which way they managed to stop him but he knew that either way it would have to be soon. It wouldn't be the first bad guy he had to kill to keep the street safe. Weeks passed and nothing happened, he was unsure whether that was a good or a bad sign. He hoped good but a part of him knew better and feared the worst.

He was right to be worried, whilst the police were waiting for 'Big Foot's next move he had been following Jack. Tracking his every move. To the point where he knew what time he started work, what time he finished, when he would work late, where he lived, that he had a son around eighteen years old and that he had a wife – a beautiful one too. He had found his next victim, the target he would aim all his hatred and revenge towards for what Jack had said. This would be 'Big Foot's way to ensure Jack would suffer for the rest of his life and he was not even going to lay a finger on him. But he was certainly going to have fun teaching his wife that her husband should be more careful about what he says, that he was wrong to goad him or to question his sexuality. He was going to make him regret what he said for the rest of his life, metaphorically cutting his heart out.

Chapter 21

By August of 2007, Joseph Darko had killed fifty nine people. Fifty nine squares on his battered chess board had been branded with an x. He was now working as a cleaner and occasional night porter in a hostel in Moscow city centre east of Red Square. After he was fired from working in the supermarket he had various odd jobs but eventually found this job and had been working there for the past three years. In work he was always very polite and kept to himself. Although his fellow co-workers knew little about him they found him an amicable individual. His bosses liked him; he was always on time, never sick and kept the place spotless. He was primarily responsible for washing the windows, cleaning the floors and toilets every day in all the hostel rooms and keeping the reception area tiny. He did not have to make the beds or dust the furniture – that was the job of the maid Nikita, a small, plump woman who had been there longer than any other member of staff. No one was quite sure how long and nobody dared ask her. Despite her stature she had a caustic personality and nobody, not even the managers of the hotel, wanted to get onto the wrong end of her venomous tongue. Well into her sixties her hair was always in rollers covered by a head scarf. She and Joseph rarely spoke but when they did he was careful to remain polite and not to reveal his latent extant dark side to her. Early on when he started working there he considered killing her but decided against it – people would miss her, start to ask questions. He did not need such heat at the time but he would not rule out killing her in the future.

Since arriving in Moscow Joseph had killed fifty five people and was well on his way to achieving his goal of killing sixty four – one for every square on his hated father's chess board. Originally the catalyst for his killing spree was the unfortunate accidental death of his mother; he had set out on a revenge mission against the world to avenge the misfortune that had befallen him and had shattered his meagre yet blissful existence in the countryside on the outskirts of Volgograd. Now years after that event (although he still thought often with heartfelt affection for his beloved mother) his motives were now very different. He began to crave killing. He became addicted to it. He was unsure whether it was the killing he craved or the sense of achievement (something he had never felt in his life) that he gained from filling in another x on the chess board, each one bringing him closer to his ultimate goal.

Increasingly the misanthrope saw human beings and human life as beneath him; worthless. He began to see little or no value in people's lives. He felt human flesh had only as much value as sausage meat and one less filthy pig on the street was as much a service to society as anything else.

By killing the people he did and ending, as he saw it, their futile existence on this earth he felt like he was not only helping society but also helping those that he killed. He felt like he was moving them on to another life, opening a door to another world, a world where they could start anew, maybe they would make a better go of life the second time around than they had the first time. This defunct thought process made him begin to see himself as a father to those he killed – as if, in some twisted way, he had actually given birth to his victims by killing them.

Whether he truly even believed this was something he was unsure of but one thing that he was sure of, was that since he had arrived in Moscow the feeling that he was better than other human's bubbled inside him to the point where there was now no debate – he was better that all those around him. A god amongst insects and his self-aggrandising attestations of how in some macabre way, he gave birth to his victims, only solidified this rational in his head.

The first time he heard of Vitali Chikalito was when he arrived in Moscow. Ever since then Joseph had become obsessed by the man and his 'achievements', as he put it, of being the most notorious serial killer of all in Russian history. By now he had already surpassed the number of murders Chikalito had claimed to have committed and he was by no means finished. Even when he eventually did reach sixty four his thirst for death would likely mean that he would continue on.

During Joseph's time in Moscow his obsession for Chikalito grew to the point that daily he would talk aloud to his 'murder mentor'. After a while he was having full blown conversations with Chikalito until eventually Chikalito was actually the one instigating the conversations with Joseph and not the other way around as had previously been the case. Joseph thought of Chikalito as the big brother he never had – someone who would always look out for him.

Originally Joseph would question what would Chikalito do in certain situations, then that evolved into Chikalito telling Joseph how he would react in certain situations until eventually, around victim number thirty eight Chikalito started to coerce and inculcate Joseph to kill certain people in certain ways.

Though ever since Joseph had surpassed Chikalito's figure of fifty six victims, he suddenly started to become critical of Joseph, something he had never done previously. Up to that point he had been nothing but supportive but as soon as Joseph marked square number fifty six on his chess board with his mother's lip stick there was a significant change in their, until then, brotherly relationship.

Initially it was small things Chikalito would be critical of, but by victim number fifty nine Chikalito was criticising Joseph's victim selection, location selection, his less than fecund killing methods and recently he had started to even question Joseph's status as a 'god'.

Joseph tried to ignore it. He cherished his 'elder brother' and although he would never say so to his face, he put Chikalito's criticisms down to jealousy on his part; that he had proven that he was better that the previously perceived most notorious serial killer in Russia.

Chapter 22

Several weeks after Jack's infamous soliloquy, on a Thursday night, around 8:00 pm when he knew, having traced his every movement for some time, that Jack would be working late; until at least 10 or 10:30 pm. 'Big Foot' drove his run down black Dodge Charger out to Jack Wolfe's neighbourhood and parked across from where Jack lived. He knew his wife would be alone in the house.

He got out of the car, pulled his large khaki hood right over his face, covering his eyes, swung his old Donnay tennis racket bag, which contained his axe, over his shoulder and closed the car door behind him. He stood there motionless for a full minute, starring at the house of his next victim. The light in the upstairs bedroom came on. An ominous smile formed over his stubbly haggard visage – unleashing his small yellow crooked teeth. He made his way towards the house, dragging his right leg as he moved. He had injured it whilst killing his first victim; his axe slipped out of his hands and as he swung the fatal blow upon his victim, the axe fell directly onto his ankle, cutting into it, badly damaging it. He never went to see anyone about it or even treated it himself and it had become badly infected. The pain in his leg grew by the day and permeated around his body.

As he reached the back door of the house he no longer noticed any pain. His adrenaline was pumping, he was excited about what he was about to do and more so how his actions would emotionally destroy Lieutenant Jack Wolfe. He broke the glass of the back door, put his hand into the space he had just fashioned, turned the lock, opened the door and entered the house. As he stood in the unlit kitchen he could hear water running upstairs. She is having a bath he thought to himself. The disgusting smile, he had on his face moments ago, returned. He walked through the kitchen into the hallway, past the living room and stood there at the bottom of the stairs. None of the lights downstairs were on but the light on the upstairs landing was. He slowly made his way up the stairs, creating as little noise as he could manage. His hood was still covering his eyes. As he reached the top of the stairs, a quick survey of the area revealed Jack's son's room to his right and to his left was Jack and his wife's room. To the left of that, at the end of the hallway was the bathroom, steam coming from underneath its door as the water ran.

As Aishling lay in the bath, he approached. Outside the door he could hear Jack's wife humming some song that he had never heard of. He moved the tennis racket bag around from behind him until it was resting in between his chest and his stomach. He slowly pulled the zip back to reveal the fireman's axe which lay sleeping in the bag. He looked down on it like a doting father upon a baby. Time to wake up, he thought, time to do some damage. He picked the axe out of the Donnay bag with his right hand, zipped it back up again and replaced the empty bag behind his back again.

He tapped on the door of the bathroom and said aloud in a voice that almost sang "Mrs Wolfe – I'm going to kill you now…". "Jack? Jack is that you? came the reply. He smirked, no it's not your pig of a husband you stupid bitch he thought to himself.

He burst through the door and removed his hood to reveal his psychotic face. Through the steam which filled the room Aishling could make out a huge, almost demonic figure, standing in the doorway of the bathroom. He was so much taller than Jack, was her initial thought, which was the pre-cursor for the blinding fear that enveloped every nerve in her body. As the shadowy figure rushed towards her with a large metallic object raised right about his head she let out a scream – a scream for help, for Jack, for anyone… 'Big Foot' rained down blows upon her whilst she flailed and thrashed in the bathtub. When he had finished the water was red. The screaming had stopped. He turned off the hot water tap which remained running throughout. As the door to the bathroom was open there was now no longer any steam in the room. He looked down on the Aishling's now lifeless body that lay before him and despite being covered in blood he was still struck by how pretty his victim was.

He bent down, grabbed Aishling's hair with his left hand and lifted her up out of the water until they were face to face, her shins banging against the side of the tub. Her arms drooped by her side, her eyes closed. He looked at her, smiled and swung the axe which had remained in his right hand the whole time and lopped her head clean off.

Her decapitated body crashed back into the crimson water. 'Big Foot' turned and headed for the door, eyes fixed on Aishling's face, not bothering to turn around to observe the destruction he had left in his wake he slowly and quietly made his way down stairs just as carefully as he had done on his way up.

He put his axe back in his bag and swung it around onto his back. Before taking one last look at Aishling's face he put her head inside his jacket and exited the house the same way he had come in, gently closing the door behind him. As he walked he fantasised about how great the head would look in a jar of formaldehyde, taking pride of place in his fridge alongside the other 'murder memento's' he had acquired since starting his killing spree.

When he reached his car, he placed the tennis racket case in through the open passenger seat window, opened the trunk of his car and reverently took the head from inside his jacket and placed it inside. Just as he was closing the boot he said aloud "that will teach you dirty pig to mess with me'. As he walked to the driver's door, he turned, faced the house and again said aloud "wonder what tough words you gonna have for me now pig?" With that he got into the car and slowly drove off, observing the stop sign at the end of the street, before continuing on his way back home.

When Jack returned home later that night around 10:45pm he had no idea of the horror which was awaiting him upstairs. As he opened the front door he called out to his wife, to let her know he was home. When he received no answer he assumed she must have fallen asleep waiting for him to arrive home. As he put his briefcase down something caught his eye in the kitchen. He looked and noticed that the back door window was broken. "AISHLING!?" he called. Still no answer. He started to worry. He withdrew his gun from its holster, cocked it and raced upstairs, calling out for his wife. When he reached the top of the stairs a quick look to his left and he could see that the bathroom door had been smashed open. As he made his way toward it he called out again for his wife to answer him. He tentatively stepped forward, longing for the deafening silent to be shattered by Aishling's sweet voice. As he moved forward with trepidation he began to pray that everything would be ok, that she would be ok.

When he entered the bathroom he had to do a double take as he was not certain what he was actually looking at. When he managed to ascertain the full horror of what lay before him he could barely process it. He fell to his knees and puked up all over the bathroom floor. His whole world was over. He had an excruciating pain in his heart, his stomach, his hands were vigorously trembling and his head was spinning. The one thought he managed to formulate was that at least Luke was safe with his grandparents; as he was spending the week with them in North Carolina.

Just then there was a buzzing in his left trouser pocket. He could just about figure out that it was his phone ringing. As if on auto pilot he answered it, wiping away the excess vomit that has formed around the edge of his mouth.

"We got 'em sir" came the voice on the other end of the line. "We got that sick son of a bitch!". "What?", "Who is this?" Jack managed to spurt out. "Sir, it's me, Redondo, Detective Redondo. 'Big Foot' ran a red light near the Brooklyn bridge as he was being flagged down by a patrol car on a routine stop and search. When he failed to stop the patrol car engaged in pursuit. It seems that sick bastard aint much of a driver cause after just a few minutes of being chased he almost flipped the car, managed to regain control of it again only to smash into a parked Mac Ten truck trailer." Detective Redondo continued to recount how the perusing officers had surrounded the car, guns drawn. The drivers head was lying against the wheel sounding the horn. The officers assumed he was dead. They called him until he came to. When he did, he lashed out and grabbed the officer with his left hand, which had been leaning in the driver's window trying to wake him up. With his right hand he fumbled for his axe that was on the passenger seat. As soon as the officer's partner saw the axe in 'Big Foot's' hand a barrage of shots rang out and he killed him whilst he sat in the driver's seat. The left hand, which had a hold of the officer, went limp and 'Big Foot' lay back in the driver's seat mouth open, face pointing towards the roof of the car, hood still covering his eyes.

"They tell me he had some pretty freaky shit in the boot of his car sir, maybe you should get down there and have a look for yourself. I hear they found some body parts and even a decapitated head…" Detective Redondo continued.

Jack had been in a daze whilst Redondo had recounted what had happened, the only thing he really managed to pick up was that 'Big Foot' was dead but as soon as he had heard 'decapitated head' he became fully lucid again and the phone fell out of his now limp hand away from his face and smashed on the bathroom floor.

Chapter 23

Jack never made it to the crime scene that night, never confirmed for himself that it was actually 'Big foot' who had been killed, never looking into the trunk of his car to observe its horrific contents, never confirmed to himself that it actually contained Aishling's decapitated head. He never made it back to work again. He couldn't. He physically could not bring himself to do it; he felt paralysed by the events that had befallen him.

His whole world had ended. Jack was meant to act as an aegis for his wife instead he had goaded 'Big Foot' into avenging his rash comments and as such endangering her. 'Big Foot's actions had plunged him into a darkness that he could not see a way out of or even any point in trying to. Aishling received a full policemen's funeral with a lone piper leading the cortège of Jack's entire precinct in mourning her death. In a way they knew that they were also mourning his death because the Jack they knew was no more and deep down they suspected that he would never return to be a New York cop again.

Aishling's parents took care of all the

funeral arrangements. From the moment Luke had returned from staying with them in North Carolina, to find the full extent of the horror that had befallen his beloved mother, he refused to speak to his father. He blamed him for what had happened, for taunting 'Big Foot' into his actions, into killing his mother in order to exact revenge upon his father. No matter how much Jack tried to talk to Luke, to break down the wall he had erected between them, it made no difference. He got no response. He eventually realised his efforts were futile and would remain so. This realisation plunged him even deeper into the depths of depressions. Aishling's parents tried to persuade Luke that it was not his father's fault - that he was just doing his job; trying to make the streets safer, trying to catch a killer that was terrorising the city and that 'Big Foot' was a psychopath – there was no logical or rational motive behind his actions.

Their efforts made little difference. After his mother's funeral Luke went to live with his grandparents in North Carolina. They were reluctant to take him because they wanted him to stay with his father and work things out, but they also knew that he was grieving for his mother and maybe over time he would be able to realise that it was not his dad who was to blame for his mother's death - 'Big Foot' was - and that he could reconcile his differences with him and they could live together again.

Luke was not the only one who felt his dad was responsible for getting Aishling killed. Jack also felt the same; he could barely look at himself in the mirror. He had a constant sickly feeling in his stomach and an empty feeling in his heart. He felt useless; like his life no longer had any purpose. Everything in the house reminded him of Aishling, which made him feel guilty for what had happened and angry that 'Big Foot' was dead – that he had not been the one to kill him. If he had, he would have made him suffer, suffer agonising pain. But he knew that no matter how much he would have hurt or tortured him he would never make him suffer a fraction of the pain he was experiencing right now – you have to love to feel such pain, such loss. 'Big Foot' was only ever consumed by hate. Any physical pain Jack could inflict upon 'Big Foot' would only scratch the surface in relation to the emotional hell Jack was going through.

He decided to make a drastic change, he could no longer stay in the house he had spent his entire marital life in with Aishling; it simply hurt too much. He decided he would move to Russia, to Moscow. Partly so he could get away from everything that reminded him of his beloved deceased wife and his only son who would no longer acknowledge his own fathers existence, but also he wanted to move to the other side of the world - to an environment that was completely alien to him as much as a personal punishment than anything else. It would represent a form of self-flagellation, to move to his own personal gulag, to make amends for his actions which many (including himself) felt resulted in Aishling's eventual murder. In Moscow he would live out the rest of his days in solitude, away from the support system he had back in back in New York in his neighbours, his friends and work colleagues, he did not want them to try to make him feel better. In his eyes, he deserved to be miserable and by going to a place like that he was certain he would be. There he would drink himself to death and suffer every day doing so, as a form of penance, in the hope that when he met Aishling again in the next world she might forgive him for his brashness and stupidity in calling out 'Big Foot' which resulted in her tragically losing her life in such a horrific way.

Chapter 24

There was increasingly a direct correlation between the growth in Joseph's perception of himself as a god, his disdain for human life, his addiction to killing (and the sense of power and achievement that stemmed from it - from marking a square off on his chess board) and his confidence as a killer and the shear brutality with which he treated his later victims.

In his early days as a killer, when he arrived in Moscow, he always chose easy targets, prima facie homeless drunks. He would get them drunk on Vodka and when they were sufficiently inebriated to the point where they were relatively incapacitated he would bash them over the head with the very vodka bottle they had just been drinking from. Occasionally he would use a hammer, which he sometimes brought along with him, which he concealed in the inside pocket of his denim jacket. The murders were planned, calculated and carried out meticulously and emotionlessly.

The closer he got to achieving his goal the more he became capable of killing not just people he was planning on killing; not just easy prey and not only people he knew would not be missed and therefore he would be unlikely to be caught because the police would not investigate the matter too closely. Increasingly he became capable of killing anyone who crossed him. 'How dare these vermin not respect my superiority over them?' he would think to himself 'Who the hell are they compared to me?', 'If only they knew the power I have over them and their pathetic little lives!'.

Also, frequently the closer he got to achieving his goal of sixty four squares marked on his father's chess board with a red x painted with his mother's lip stick, the more he sought out a challenge and also the more he began to seek to engage the police in his game. His increasing hubris was resulting in a proclivity towards a certain brio when killing his victims.

Chapter 25

Without telling a soul Jack moved to Russia with only a few belongings. He did not sell the house – he would leave that to Luke when he had successfully drowned himself in a sea of alcohol.

He managed to secure a job with the Moscow police force. Despite his pidgin Russian his record was impeccable and the ill-equipped and under staffed Muscovite police force were only too delighted to have him.

As a child, Jack and the rest of his Irish Catholic family lived in the Brighton beach area of New York. Brighton beach is an area on Coney Island in the borough of Brooklyn. It was dubbed "Little Odessa" by the local populace due to many of its residents having come from Odessa. It was and still is the home of the Russian Mafia in the United States. The neighbourhood has a distinctively ethnic feel – akin to Manhattan's Chinatown. The majority of the people making up the "Russian" community are mainly Jewish immigrants from the former Soviet Union, due to the repressive policies of the Soviet government towards Jewish culture and language.

It has, and had, the largest Russian-speaking community in the United States. The primary language used in the Brighton Beach area of Brooklyn is Russian. Displays and advertisements are hung in Russian in the social and commercial hub or the area that is Brighton Beach Avenue. Russian restaurants had live entertainment featuring traditional Russian dances – people gathered at these restaurants for special occasions and did not go there just to eat, but also to dance. All these places employed only Russian speakers to deal with the solely Russian speaking clientele of the establishments. Brighton Beach is the cornerstone of the Russian community in America. As such the Irish Catholic Wolfe family's presence there was something of an anomaly.

Although they stood out as being different, their Russian Jewish neighbours embraced them into the community and as a boy Jack could understand quite a lot of Russian – he had to in order to even buy groceries in the shops in the neighbourhood. He and his older brother Sean would often have to accompany their parents whenever they were going to the grocery store or to the pharmacy (of which there was one on every street corner) or the butcher shop or just about anywhere they might have to converse. Neither of the boy's parents could understand or speak much Russian at all so it was up to either Jack or Sean to do all the talking and translating when it came to the weekly commercial transactions. The local shop owners all spoke Russian and were very warm and welcoming to the Wolfe family. They became well versed to conducting conversations with the children of the family as opposed to, as they normally would for all their other customers, with the parents.

Jack had many friends in the neighbourhood and would communicate in Russian to them. He was not fluent and understood far more than he could speak; often he would speak in English and his Russian/American friends would speak in their mother tongue – that way both parties were at ease in the own languages. Equally sometimes Jack would try and speak in Russian whilst his friends would try and speak in English; this way both had to make an effort to understand the other and both parties were learning.

When Jack was twelve years old his grandmother (his father's mother) died, leaving them a three bedroom house with a front and back garden in the Bronx. It represented a big improvement from their current two bedroom apartment. They moved from Brighton beach and Jack and his brother Sean, despite their best efforts, eventually lost touch with their Russian/American friends they had there.

Now in his mid-forties Brighton Beach seemed like a lifetime ago for Jack. When he arrived in Moscow he had not even heard Russian, let alone spoken it, in over thirty years. So having to live in Moscow would represent a tortuous and arduous challenge. That was exactly was he wanted though; partly to punish himself and partly to vainly try to get his mind off his recently deceased wife until he managed to kill himself. This was the absolute nadir of his life.

Chapter 26

42 was an uncalculated yet particularly violent killing. It was a dark and murky Wednesday night, 2:30 am. It had been raining heavily all day and had just recently stopped. The streets glistened with freshly fallen rain as Joseph walked home from 'Red Star', a bar close to Hotel Europa where he sometimes drank. He had consumed a few glasses of Vodka, nothing serious. He was not drunk and as he walked his mind wandered to the Who? When? Where? and with What? of his next victim. As he played out various death scenes in his head he came to a set of traffic lights. He had decided he would walk the fifteen or so minutes back home. The streets were deserted and he liked them when they were like that.

As he began to cross the road, a dark parked car (a taxi) which was waiting for the lights to change, started to rev its engine. Joseph awoke from his gruesome daze, he was half way across the street by now and the green man was still beckoning him to continue crossing the road. 'Don't test me you prick' Joseph thought to himself as he starred at the green light in front of him as he walked, fixating on an image of the taxi driver in his mind's eye.

Suddenly the lights changed as Joseph was still only half way across the road, as if the taxi driver was oblivious to the moving obstacle that was obstructing his way, he slammed on the accelerator. Joseph was forced to leap out of the way of the oncoming vehicle. He was momentarily shocked. 'What the hell is the matter with this guy?', 'He nearly knocked me down', 'He tried to knock me down... he tried to kill me!'.

As he hit the floor he looked up to see the speeding taxi was slowing down. Joseph looked slightly further down the street to see the reason why – the light, just a hundred meters from where Joseph was lying, was turning orange.

That was all Joseph needed to see. It was like a red flag to a bull. He jumped to his feet and ran as fast as he could towards the now stationary car. 'You are dead my friend!' he whispered aloud to himself as he ran. Unbuttoning his denim jacket, as he ran, he withdrew his hammer. It was over 12 inches long with a thick, heavy 3 x 2 inch solid head atop of it.

Only meters away from the taxi, the driver was starting to rev his engines again in anticipation of an imminent green light. As he arrived at the taxi he smashed its back window with the hammer, without stopping for a second he ran to the driver's door, opened it and grabbed the driver by the neck with his left hand. "What is your pro…?" the taxi driver started to say. Joseph cut him off. He pushed his face mere inches away from the taxi drivers, still maintaining his grip with his left hand, fangs visible he growled "Can you see me now? Do you see me now? You asshole!" he screamed as saliva drooled down the edges of his mouth. The taxi driver went pale. Without waiting for a response, hammer in his right hand, Joseph smashed blow after blow onto the head of the taxi driver until his victim lost consciousness.

He awoke to the sound of a revving engine. In a daze, the taxi driver looked up. He was now tied to a lamp post in an area he did not recognise. Joseph had taken him to an abandoned industrial estate he had discovered near Bittsa Park.

As he came to, he could see his taxi around ten feet in front of him. All the windows had been smashed out. At the wheel was the person he had nearly knocked down earlier.

The taxi driver – 5,11" Gregori Rebrov, a single man in his early forties, was a mean spirited man who was also completely bald. He was wearing what he always wore whilst on duty - the same jeans, white vest and leather waistcoat combination. Which meant he all too frequently stank of body odour and so in turn, did his taxi. He was tied by his hands and feet to the pole. He tried to loosen his bonds; to squeeze free but it was pointless. All he could hear was the engine of his taxi revving ferociously. He looked up and made eye contact with Joseph.

- "So you finally woke up you ugly prick".
- "No please, I'm sorry, I was wrong, I should not have done it. Please let me go, I'm sorry".

It was starting to get bright again, the day was dawning. Gregori guessed from his many years of working the night shift it was nearly six o clock.

- "You see me now do you? Do you asshole?" Joseph said, berating his victim for his earlier transgression when he almost ran him over with his taxi.
- "I'm sorry" pleaded Gregori.
- "Try and jump out of the way of this…!"

With that Joseph removed his foot from the break and the car speed toward Gregori. One last time he squirmed to break free but it was a fruitless endeavour. As the car surged towards its target Joseph was hunched up at the wheel, eyes wide, unflinchingly fixed on his victim, savouring every squirming motion, every cry for help, his teeth were clenched together revealing a twisted smile.

"Take that, you bastard!" he yelled as he smashed the car onto the pole Gregori was tied to. He was killed instantly. Joseph undid his seat belt. Fragments of glass were lodged in the side of his face and neck. A trickle of blood flowed down his face from a cut over his right eyebrow. He left the driver's door open as he exited the car, walked up to the now dead Gregori and screamed into his lifeless face "See me now?! Do you see me now?" With that he calmly turned on his heels and walked away from his latest victim. He casually made his way to Bittsa Park metro station some fifteen minutes' walk away and waited for the first train to arrive at 6:30 am.

Chapter 27

Luke enrolled in North Carolina University in the autumn of the year his mother was slain. Since moving there after his mother's death, he had used her maiden name as his surname and no longer went by 'his former' surname Wolfe. He never discussed the subject of his father with his classmates, nor despite their best efforts, with his grandparents. He transferred from N.Y.U. to N.C.U. after his first year and started up classes in September with the same course he had majored in at N.Y.U. – Arts & Languages. His new Arts lecturer was not a patch on his mother; she could illuminate and enliven a topic to the point where the entire lecture room would wait with bated breath, on the edge of their seats, for what she would say next. His new lecturer, Dr Ted Fielding was childlike in stature; he looked like a twelve year old boy. He had round rimmed glasses and his appearance had earned him the moniker 'Harry Potter'. Yet despite his meek appearance he had a fierce temper and did not encourage questions during his lectures. He handed out notes at the beginning of each lecture and simply read them aloud to the lecture room, to no one in particular, in perfect soporific mono tone.

Luke tried not to compare him with his mother (there was no contest), instead he tried to just buckle down and get on with things – to build a new life for himself in North Carolina as best he could.

Despite quickly acquiring many friends, Luke lived off campus with his grandparents. They could not afford for him to stay on campus and Luke did not really mind; if it meant that he did not have to ask his father for money he would gladly sacrifice living on Campus with his friends. When his classmates questioned why he did not choose to live in the student accommodation on campus he said that both his parents were dead and his grandparents liked him to be in the house as they felt safe with him there.

Luke's grandparents, Aidan and Rita Callaghan, were in their late 60's. Luke often thought that his grandfather must have been a big man in his prime as he was just over 6,1" and was still quite stocky for his age. Of course at his age he now had the luggage of a pot belly that he had to carry around with him. He wore round framed glasses, was always clean shaven and despite greying significantly at the sides had a brilliant streak of red hair on top of his head.

Rita was little over 5 foot. A rotund woman, who has a perpetually cheery demeanour which resulted in her having a smile on her face continuously thus accentuating the roundness of her cheeks. Aishling clearly got her plump round cheeks from her mother, Jack always thought whenever he saw Rita.

They lived a mile outside of the city of Charlotte in North Carolina in a two bedroom house with a porch out front where a white swing chair resided with enough room for the two of them to sit and watch the world pass by.

Aidan and Rita had an enormous back garden where Luke's grandfather grew just about every fruit or vegetable imaginable; from beetroot to broccoli, cabbage to carrots. Aidan had a huge fridge in the pantry where he bagged it all when it was ready and stored it for whenever they wanted anything.

When the opportunity arose during Luke's second semester in N.C.U. to study abroad for his third year he jumped at the chance. The fee worked out as roughly the same as a year in his current university - so his grandparents would not have to pay any extra if he was chosen to go.

There were only six places and the majority of his fifty classmates had expressed an interest in going so he felt his chances of actually going abroad where very slim. Much to his surprise and delight he was chosen as one of the six to study abroad for a year. Although he was not the best in his class he was extremely dedicated to his studies and his efforts did not go unnoticed with the selection committee. He had never missed a class (no matter what time they were scheduled) even though he would have to travel for at least an hour to get home afterwards. Sometimes he would not get home until 10 or 10:30 at night – after being in college all day he would just go straight to bed, rise again early the next morning to start all over again. The selection committee were aware that he lived off campus and what time he must have been getting home and arriving at college for the last lectures at night and the first ones in the morning. This dedication was one of the principal reasons he was chosen to be one of the six to do their third year studies abroad.

The options were to go to either France, Spain, Denmark or Finland. If he chose either Denmark or Finland he would be doing all his lectures in English, he could not see the point of doing this, so instantly dismissed these as possible destinations. Which left Spain and France, Spanish and French – his major and minor languages respectively, in his Arts and Languages course. These two options would result in all lectures being conducted in either one of these languages for the full year – there would be no English modules. A daunting prospect seeing as he would be required to take all his third year exams in either subject. As he had a better level of Spanish than French he decided that the option of one year studying in the Andalucian city of Granada was the option that best suited him.

When he was selected he was thrilled and when he told his grandparents they were delighted also – they hoped that a year abroad might give him a new perspective on life, make him a little bit more mature and in turn might make him more inclined to start talking to his father again.

The summer before he left for Spain, he worked as much as he could at any odd job he could get – he did some landscaping work for his grandparents' neighbours, washed cars, walked dogs, babysat, anything to earn some extra cash. Primarily he worked in a Carls Junior fast food restaurant - working as many shifts as possible. He did not go out or socialise with his friends the entire summer because he did not want to spend any money. By the time he was leaving for Spain near the end of the summer he had amassed over $4,000 (well over €3,000) and as Southern Spain was supposedly a lot cheaper to live than America and coupled with the fact that he would not have a car over there he was fairly confident he would be able to last a long time on the money he had saved and when he eventually did start to run out he figured he could always get a job teaching English.

Chapter 28

49 was a more calculated yet equally violent killing. As he neared his ultimate goal a cockiness that was not present when he first started killing in Moscow was now very evident.

Of the homeless drunks that called Bittsa Park home some stayed for a short time, others remained for a lot longer. Up to this point Joseph had carefully selected those who were only in the park a short time, those who did not know any of the 'residents' of the park. He would befriend them, buy their company with a cheap bottle of vodka, all for the price of having to endure stories of his beloved dog Dragan. Sometimes he would discuss the dog from his childhood, other times he would discuss the one that he meet when he first moved to Moscow. He never mentioned how they actually came to their demise, only that this beloved dog died of old age and whichever drunk was about to become his next victim would drink a mouthful of vodka with Joseph, in the dog's honour.

After the bottle was finished and they were quite drunk and helpless, Joseph would smash their heads in with the bottle. This evolved to bashing their heads in with a hammer, which later evolved into bashing a gaping hole into his victim's head and wedging the empty vodka bottle into it.

With his next victim, this evolutionary line of killing methods took a macabre and horrific leap forward. Originally, and up to this point, he had killed homeless drunks that nobody really knew and as such they would not be missed. His next victim though would definitely be someone that would be missed and he knew as much – that was why he was picking him.

The reason he picked him was that he had seen on the news and read in Tvoi Dyen the previous day that 'the Bittsa Park Maniac had been caught'. Joseph was disgusted. Some patient who had escaped from the psychiatric hospital in Bittsa Park was claiming responsibility for his masterpieces. He claimed responsibility for the sixteen murders that the police were attributing to 'the Maniac'.

Joseph wanted to promulgate to Moscow that he was still very much at large, a caveat to strike fear into the hearts of Muscovites and not just to those who lived in the Bittsa Park neighbourhood, who had been elated that the killer that had terrorised the area for so long had been caught. His next victim would prove otherwise.

'Black tooth' as he was known by all those who lived in the park, had been living homeless in Bittsa park longer than any other homeless drunks who currently frequented it. He had acquired the name as he was missing all but a few teeth and the ones he did possess were all completely rotten. He was perceived as somewhat of the benevolent ruler of Bittsa Park. As he had been there longer than anyone else he had gained a certain degree of gravitas amongst his peers. He was a little uncomfortable with his mock title but his fellow homeless drunks were merely letting it be known that they held him in high esteem.

Even he could not quite remember what age he was, over fifty five in anyway, he was sure of that (in actual fact he was closer to sixty five). He measured 5,3", bald on the top of his head with bushy grey hair at the sides. He had a round face, big cheeks and a pig like nose. Despite his ominous name he was very softly spoken. He always wore three coats, even in the summer months and a pair of fingerless gloves.

Joseph knew all about him, he had heard about him from many of his victims. They had mentioned him, mentioned that he was helping them find a dry place to sleep. Joseph had steered well clear of him up to this point. He had not wanted to attract that much attention. Now though making a big scene, getting people to notice him, his masterpiece was exactly what he sought.

'Black tooth' like most of the homeless in Bittsa Park was an alcoholic, but Joseph knew that he would never touch 'dirty vodka' as such he knew in order to cajole him into drinking with him he would have to bring a more expensive bottle than he usually would for his victims. He bought a bottle for 250 roubles, treble what he would usually spend. He managed to find 'Black tooth', waited for him to be on his own, approached him and asked would he like to drink with him. As soon as 'Black tooth' saw the prestigious *marque* on the bottle he was more than willing to.

Joseph brought him to a secluded

area of the park 'where he had buried he beloved dog dragan' he said. He wanted to drink a drink in his honour and wanted some company. 'Black tooth' was more concerned with getting his lips around the expensive bottle his new friend had bought, than the location they would be drinking it or who they would be drinking it in honour of.

'Black tooth' was a victim of Joseph's like any other homeless drunk; he drank with him, he told stories about Dragan to him, he waited for the bottle to be finished and bashed his head in with it, he even bashed a hole in 'black tooths' head with a hammer and when he had made a big enough crater he stuck the empty bottle into it. That, up to that point, had been the extent of Joseph's cruelty towards his victims in the park. Although this was not where he stopped with 'Black tooth'.

He took out sixteen two inch nails – one for every victim that the police and media had accused the so called 'Bittsa Park Maniac' of killing. One by one he hammered the two inch long nails into the face of 'Black tooth'. Eights nails one and a half inches deep under each of his eyes. By the time he had finished, 'black tooth' was truly unrecognisable, his face looked like a ten axle truck had run over it. There was blood everywhere.

By the time he had finished it was 7:30 pm on a sunny summer's evening, there would just be enough time for Joseph to get the metro home, change clothes and be at the hostel in time to start his shift as a night porter – not before he marked off the forty ninth square on his chessboard of course.

Chapter 29

Luke loved life in Granada. He was enrolled in La Universidad de Granada, a college which was tiny compared to his former colleges of N.Y.U. and even N.C.U. back in the States. It took him only ten minutes to walk to class from his apartment which he shared with his roommates Mathew and Jean Paul.

There were a lot of Americans at the University but Luke made an effort not just to socialise with them; he tried to also hang around with the other foreign students from around the world that were also studying at the University – mostly Europeans, primarily from England and France but also some Dutch and Italians. Hanging out with Spaniards proved more difficult though. They were less open to making the inevitable effort that was required with a foreigner to include them in Spanish life and to integrate them into their group of friends. Luke did not blame them for it - would he be any more welcoming of a foreigner on campus back home? Sure he would be friendly, but would he invite them out with his friends? He was not so sure. Yet he did lament the feeling that he was not making the most out of his Spanish experience.

He wanted to soak up more Spanish culture and particularly improve his ability to speak the language.

In the first semester (which he spent with a *madre*) he barley learnt any new vocabulary. He virtually made no effort at all – he was too busy partying. In the second semester (which he was now spending living in apartment 5C, calle San Anton with Mathew and Jean Paul he tried to have more of a mix. He would try to study and learn as much as possible; do *intercambios* with Spanish students whereby they would speak English and he would speak Spanish. He would do that Monday to Thursday then from Thursday evening to Saturday night/Sunday morning he would get more drunk that he ever had before in his life. He would recover and recharge on Sunday and on Monday he would start all over again.

Luke also had managed to acquire a Spanish girlfriend, Laura, since having moved to 5C. She was a friend of Jean Paul's whom he had met in Semester one. Laura was about 5,2", slight figure, curly dyed blonde hair. She was virtually always dressed in jeans and her beat up Adidas gazelle sized four and a half runners. Luke liked her a lot and the best thing was that Mathew and Jean Paul thought she was great too. Despite frequently having a Spanish woman in the apartment, the amount of Spanish spoken there did not increase much. When they were drinking (every Thursday, Friday, Saturday) they were having too much fun to worry about speaking the language and besides Laura spent two months working in a pub in Cornwall in England, the previous summer so she could easily communicate in English.

No matter what they did or where they went, the night was never complete for Luke until he had eaten a shawarma and drunk dry a brand new bottle of rum he had bought for the night's festivities.

As much as the majority of their time was spent killing brain cells and abusing their liver Luke, Jean Paul, Mathew, Rob and Will could not be happier than when they were in one another's company. The group had started in a very ad hoc way. Matthew arrived in Granada in Semester two and started hanging around with Jean Paul's friends, which he had met in semester one. They would traditionally congregate back at Tariq's apartment, a Moroccan in his late twenties, where they would share a bottle of Vodka which Tariq would buy. The bottle would be shared between the hundred and twenty five people (or so it seemed to Matthew) who would turn up to the apartment on such nights. Matthew never really enjoyed these nights, not just because he never had enough alcohol to get drunk but also because he found Tariq (who spoke perfect English) very rude towards him. He never felt welcome there and he never felt at ease around Traiq. He met Rob and Will at one such party in the apartment. They had just arrived from America a few weeks before and were at the party as guests of one of Tariq's friends.

Matthew instantly clicked with the two and eventually between themselves they managed to change the dynamic of the party culture of the whole group. Party central became Matthew and Jean Paul's place. Rob and Will were always in situ and when Luke moved in he was the same. As alcohol was so cheap everyone brought their own bottle. The goal was always to finish a bottle each in one night – if you did not succeed it was no big deal but at least there was none of the 'ridiculousness' as Matthew put it regarding having only one or one and a half drinks over the course of a night – which was a typical party in Tariq's.

As Rob was meeting his brother in Madrid to travel around Europe for Spring break, Will's parents were going to be coming to Granada as a departure point for a tour around Spain, Matthew was going back to Dublin to see his family, friends and girlfriend and Luke's girlfriend Laura was going to San Sebastian for a few days with her parents. That then left Luke and Jean Paul with no plans for Spring break. They did not want to just stay in Granada, but they were unsure what they wanted to do and where they wanted to go.

Luke left it up to Jean Paul to do some research on the internet about potential destinations. After a few days he had come up with two suggestions for Holiday destinations – "The Netherlands or Russia".
- "Why the Netherlands man?"
- "Cause we can go to Amsterdam, get stoned off our faces, check out an Ajax match and then move on to the red light district…"

Luke liked smoking weed, but for a whole week? He was not so sure; being stoned did not really suit him – he became very quiet and insular if he smoked too much and doing some window shopping in the red light district sounded cool but he knew that would be the extent of his activities there. He would not be making any purchases (or rental agreements for that matter either). He was not so sure that would be the case with Jean Paul and he did not want to feel pressured into doing something he would later regret.

- "Ok, so why Russia then?" Luke asked
- "Well the thing about Russia is I was reading some dude's blog on the internet about a trip he took in Russia – it's called 'The Vodka Trail or The Vodka Train' not sure exactly but there is definitely vodka involved anyway, I am sure of that"

Luke's ears pricked up and his eyes widened, he bit his lip trying to avoid showing blatant bias for this new option.

- "Ok, ok so what is the story with it?" Luke asked trying to stay calm and not let his excitement show.
- "Well it is a little bit more expensive that the Amsterdam trip - even if you factor in all the

prostitutes we are going to get to know…"

Luke feigned a smile. Jean Paul continued "and the trip would take a total of ten days as opposed to only the one week which we would need to spend in Amsterdam, that would mean that we would miss around two days of classes when they start back up again after Spring break is over".

- "Ok, no problem tell me more about the trip itself and not just the reasons why we should not do it".
- "Ok, Jean Paul said, (his voice a little louder that before; betraying his obvious excitement about what he was about to say) we arrive in Moscow, spend two days there checking out all the sites and stuff then we get down to business (he edged forward in his seat, staring Luke in the eyes, a grin danced on his lips as he spoke) our train departs from Moscow to St. Petersburg, continues on until we eventually reach Siberia and then on to Vladivostok – the most eastern tip of Russia. On the way back to we pass through China and Mongolia and I haven't

mentioned the best part yet, all the time we are on the train we are getting smashed on Vodka and meeting likeminded people from all over the world who are also doing the trip. We could even hang out with some Russians who are only doing part of the trip. So what do you think?"

Luke was sold, as much as it was going to be expensive it was his birthday in a few weeks' time and the money his grandparents would send him would offset the cost of the trip and this was a once in a lifetime opportunity. Trying not to favour one immediately over the other, he reversed the question back to Jean Paul, trying to quell the smile that was desperately trying to reveal itself on the right side of his mouth, unable to make eye contact he said "I don't know man, what do you think?"

The two of them sat in silence for a few moments in their otherwise deserted apartment at 1:30 pm on a strangely dull Granada day. Matthew was out doing some grocery shopping. Luke was pretty sure that Jean Paul would prefer to go to Amsterdam and despite his best efforts to highlight the benefits of Amsterdam Jean Paul had picked up on Luke's obvious preference for Moscow.

For a good twenty minutes they mulled over each option again and again, each taking turns debating the various pros and cons of each trip "but what about the prostitutes man?" Jean Paul spurted out like a geezer. After several seconds of reflection Luke countered "sure half of them come from eastern Europe, why pay an inflated price in Amsterdam when you can get the real deal, at local prices, in Moscow?" Luke hoped this would appease Jean Paul - It didn't, but after they had spent nearly an hour discussing the subject Jean Paul eventually acquiesced to Luke's tacit desire to go to Russia and to go on the Vodka Train.

- "Sure I live in France, I can go to Amsterdam anytime" Jean Paul said relenting "and going to Russia is like a once in a lifetime opportunity" now warming to the idea.
- "Yeah, yeah man" Luke said trying to retard the volcanic elation rumbling inside him. Jean Paul pretended not to notice.

- "So we are agreed then – for Spring break we are going to Russia and we are going to get wrecked on the Vodka Train"
- "Yeah man" Jean Paul said, now fully on board with the idea, (after all it really was a once in a lifetime opportunity and who better to do it with than a guy like Luke – a guy with a monstrous capacity for alcohol).

When Matthew, Rob and Will found out about Luke and Jean Paul's imminent holiday they were more than a little jealous. They wished they could go too. Jean Paul and Luke wished they could go also – the five of them together in Russia would be so much fun. "You know what man" Luke said "if the five of us went on this Vodka train trip there is a very real possibility that one of us would die from alcohol poisoning … maybe even two of us…" with that they all laughed at Luke's, slightly serious, joke due to the capacity and velocity they tended to drink when they were together. "Well have a great time lads" Matthew said "drink a bottle for us". "We will" Jean Paul and Luke said in unison. The topic was finished. With that the drinking games commenced.

Chapter 30

#57 Increasingly Chikalito began to encourage Joseph to be more adventurous with his victim selection and more so with the methods of killing he chose. He lived in a social housing complex built at the height of the Cold war - hundreds of people living on a few acres of land in rows and rows of apartment blocks. His area was very run down and there was a lot of crime there. Recently gangs of young punk kids had started terrorising the residents of the Novy Arbat neighbourhood.

The *bande* that hung around the area where Joseph lived dubbed themselves 'The Midnight Blades'. They were no different from any other gang in the area, young, no education, unruly and they had no one who cared what they did all day. In Moscow (like most modern cities) that combination meant one thing – trouble. The leader of 'The Midnight Blades' was a boy called Timur. Joseph was not sure what his full name was. He was no older than fourteen, Joseph guessed. 5,6", he had a broad and muscular physique for his age. Shaven head, skin tight with big thick black eyebrows. His left hand was deformed;

his thumb was fully formed but his figures were mere stubs. Some said he lost them holding a defective fire work too long, others that he lost them in a fight and others questioned whether he was not just born like that.

Timur was always accompanied by four or five impish henchmen. Whom each would try and outdo themselves in what they would say or do to passers-by in order to gain approval from their leader.

They hung out on the corner of Joseph's building and typically they would terrorise any old people and people younger than them who went past. They would try and make them hand over whatever possessions or money they had on them.

They never tried such a thing with Joseph, but increasingly they would make fun of him whenever he would pass by; try and stand in his way as he walked, pretend like he had struck them or direct some trite, asinine comment at him. Joseph did his best to ignore it but the more he ignored it the more they would try to get a reaction for him by pushing him more and more. 'If only they knew who I was' he would often think to himself. 'I could kill every one of them in a matter of minutes. They have such big mouths; I would like to bash their teeth in with my hammer' but he always resisted such urges.

One day Joseph was walking back home at around 5:30 pm having just finished a double shift at Hotel Europa. It had been a trying day and he was in no humour of the anticipated fatuous antics of 'the Midnight Blades'. As he turned the corner and moved towards his building he was surprised to see Timur hanging around the corner on his own. Assuming that without his gang of cheer leading homunculi Timur would be too scared to say or do anything he approached his building in a more relaxed state.

Mere feet away from his door, Timur pretended to accidentally bump into Joseph. "Very sorry sir, excuse my clumsiness" Joseph was fully aware that Timur was trying to be a nuisance. "Come on, get out of my way" Joseph said abruptly, allowing (for the first time) Timur to see a glimmer of his temper and that he was growing tired of such antics. "Yes sir, sorry again sir". Joseph brushed him to one side indifferently and proceeded forward towards the gateway to his apartment building with Timur moving in the opposite direction away from the building.

As he reached the iron gateway entrance he looked back to see Timur, now at the corner of Joseph's building some fifteen feet away smiling smugly back at him. Joseph sensed something was wrong. Without thinking, he checked if his watch was still on his wrist. It wasn't. Realising that Timur had stolen it he became incandescent with rage. This was the final straw. 'This maggot has gone too far' he thought to himself.

Timur looked up - he had been momentarily lost in another world, congratulating himself on how clever he was – to see a snarling beast (Joseph) sprinting towards him, only a couple of metres away when he managed to get his bearings and thought of trying to make an escape.

As he attempted to turn, he tripped over his own feet; so much was his shocked state, lying helpless on the ground like a wounded gazelle ready to be pounced upon by an enraged lion.

Now on top of Timur, straddling his torso, Joseph grabbed him by the ears and proceeded to bash his teenage head off the payment, again and again. He was blind with rage.

When he was satisfied that he had inflicted enough damage to ensure Timur was sufficiently discombobulated and no longer had his full capabilities about him, he grabbed him by the neck and lead him into his apartment building. He was uncomfortable extolling such punishment in broad daylight in such an open area as it was. Though happy that the streets were deserted and that nobody had witnessed what had just occurred, he slammed the large iron gate of his apartment building shut behind him.

Timur was coming to as Joseph dragged him to the stairs. 'Mister, sir, please, I'm sorry, please take your watch back, I promise we will never mess with you again!" Timur's pleaded. Joseph took back his watch and put it into his back left jean pocket.

He reached the stairs which led downstairs to the laundry room and storage areas where tenants had an individual four by four foot storage area.

Adjacent to this area was the laundry room. He threw Timur to the ground. Timur looked up at him pleadingly, on his knees, back facing the stairs, which led into darkness below. Joseph could see he was about to start to beg for mercy again. In Joseph's eyes, that point had long since passed. He smashed his size nine right boot straight into Timur's whimpering face "shut the hell up!" he yelled, as the teenage leader of 'the Midnight Blades' fell back down the stairs, banging his head on every second step on the stairwell.

When he ceased his descent his body lay slumped motionless at the foot of the stairs – the progress of his descent had only been stultified by the door which lead into the basement. Joseph was sure, pretty sure at least he was not dead but he did not much care either way though.

He calmly made his way down the stairs. At the bottom, he grabbed Timur with his left hand and opened the door in front of him with his right hand. Ignoring the rows and rows of storage areas to his left he dragged Timur's body into the laundry room.

There, along the left hand wall was a row of eight industrial tumble dryers and on the right there was the same number of industrial washing machines. The room was a twenty five foot by forty foot rectangle. It was divided by a series of tables placed down the middle of the room, for the residents to arrange their laundry on. The room had a cement floor and painted walls, the colour of which was a mixture of murky yellow and dank grey-green all in one. Sporadically the florescent lights on the ceiling would flicker of their own volition.

Joseph lifted Timur up onto one of the tables in the middle of the room. As he came to, Joseph was smiling eerily down at him.
- "You like time my boy?"
- "What? no sir, sorry".
- "Then why did you steal my watch then?"
- "Yes, eh no sorry! Please sir".
- "If you like time so much then that is exactly what I will give you".

Timur did not know how to respond but he was starting to get quite frightened. Just then he noticed what Joseph was holding in his hands – a clock. There was a circular shaped stain on the wall above Joseph's head that matched the clock's size perfectly. The clock had been on the wall so long that, when it was removed it, it revealed a bright shade of canary yellow was actually the colour painted on the walls. The circular spot was no more than twelve inches in diameter and contrasted brilliantly with the dankness of the rest of the room. The clock was there for the residents of the apartment building to time how long their laundry had been on, how long they would need to wait for it to be done and so on.

Joseph lifted the clock over his head with both hands, Timur feared that he was going to smash it straight onto him face but instead he flung it against the laundry room wall in front of him and smashed it to pieces.

Timur was unsure as to what was going on. Joseph calmly walked over to the smashed clock on the floor, picked up something and walked over to where Timur lay.
- "So you like time, huh?"
- "No sir please let me go!"

Without responding to his captives' plea for mercy, he placed Timur's right hand down on the table and tied it in place with a piece of clothing he'd taken from one of the industrial tumble dryers, so that Timur could not move. He placed a long metal rod onto Timur's exposed right wrist. Initially he was unsure what it was, but soon realised that it was one of the hands from the clock his captor had taken from the wall.

Joseph plucked his hammer from his inside pocket and proceeded to pound the clock hand into Andei's wrist. Each whack of the hammer onto the metal clock hand was greeted with a symphony of screams from Timur.

Joseph did not flinch; the basement was abandoned. No machines were running and there would not be anyone starting to do laundry at this time of the evening. At this time Joseph knew that the residents of the apartment block would be starting to prepare evening supper and besides he knew that people in his building only ever came down to the basement to do laundry in the morning.

He hammered the metal clock hand into Timur's wrist until he had pinned him to the table with it. Any attempt from his victim to move was meet with agonising pain. "Scream all you want to little man – nobody can hear you and nobody is going to come help you".

- "Let's chop his little testicles off" came a voice in the room.
- "What?" Joseph said to the new person in the room that Timur could not see, or for that matter, hear.
- "Yes let's chop his little testicles off and cook them for dinner. Thrust me they will be delicious". Chikalito whispered in Joseph's ear emerging from a shadowy corner of the room. This was the first time Chikalito has suggested such a thing to Joseph and he was very much taken aback by his murder mentors suggestion.
- "Forget it. No way. That kind of stuff is not for me".
- "How do you know of you have never tried it?" Chikalito queried Joseph coming around from behind him to stare him in the face.
- "I just... know" Joseph eventually spurted out now doing his best to block out the vermicious Chikalito's very existence in the room.

Getting back to the matter in hand, Joseph moved around to Timur's head and stood behind the teenage delinquent. "If you like time so much you should have asked me for it I will gladly give it to you". He placed the other metal hand of the clock onto Timur's forehead, in between his eyes.

Joseph looked up for his mentor's approval, which would usually be forthcoming, but this time Chikalito just looked bored. Joseph had never seen his brother act this way with him and he was unsure how to react. He decided to ignore it. His good friend was annoyed with him that he had dismissed his suggestion but he would make it up to him another time. Down came the hammer onto its metal target, slicing through his victims head with ease. Timur died instantly.

Joseph picked up Timur's body off the table after he had loosened the clock hand that had been hammered into it, pinning Timur to the table. He flung the now lifeless body into one of the industrial sized tumble driers and pressed 'On'. He left Timur's cadaver rattling around the dryer for a full three hours, as he prepared and ate his evening supper, until it was sufficiently dark outside. He then removed it and dumped it out onto the side of the street near a neighbouring apartment block.

Despite the state of his body and face, there was nobody to miss him so when the police discovered Timur's body they just put in down to a particularly violent killing amongst rival gangs and did not even bother investigating the crime. Also as the crime did not take place in Bittsa Park the police had no reason to associate it with the so called 'Bittsa Park Maniac'.

Chapter 31

Jack found his new life in Russia hard – suitably hard. He lived in a one bedroom apartment on a narrow cobbled stone street just over two miles (fifteen minutes by car – he never walked) from the Lubyanka police headquarters. His partner, Pavel Mostovoi offered to find him something better; in a nicer part of the city but Jack politely refused. Mostovoi knew that on Jack's salary, which although was not substantial, he could afford something far nicer. He could never understand why Jack would want to live in such a dingy place.

Mostovoi liked Jack– he did not know much about him other than he used to be a New York cop. He knew nothing of his family life, his background. Did he have a wife or kids? He often wondered, yet did not want to pry as Jack had never offered up such details. Jack was almost always suffering from a hangover but that never concerned Mostovoi too much; some of his other work colleagues were all too often the same.

Despite minimal levels of conversing between the two, Mostovoi recognised a good man when he saw one and he knew he could see that Jack was one – and a great cop, even thought he was barley interested in most of the cases they worked on together. Often without even having read the case file he could help move a case forward immeasurably. Whether it was pure luck or instinct borne out of years of experience Jack almost always managed to make a significant contribution to the cases they worked together – almost despite himself.

Mostovoi noted that he took no pleasure from doing it. He would walk around the precinct like a zombie half the time but when he and Mostivoi were out on patrol, when it was just the two of them, Jack would open up a little more.

By contrast Marat Usmanov, the captain of the precinct and Jack's boss, did not like Jack and in particular he did not like his methods of getting the job done one little bit. He longed for a reason to fire him but the chief of police liked the idea of an American cop with a fearsome reputation and impeccable record working for the Muscovite police force. It was good for the public relations that a great American cop would want to work for the police force of Moscow.

Also, as Jack and his partner invariably solved the cases they were assigned to, Usmanov had little grounds to dismiss Jack. Yet that did not stop him from trying. He tried to make Jack's life miserable; tried to make him break so he would quit of his own volition. He would confront him in the corridor randomly and start screaming at him at the top of his lungs about anything and everything. It never had much of an effect on Jack– whilst Usmanov would yell at Jack, his eyes would glaze over and he would stare off into the distance until Usmanov grew tired and let him on his way again.

Part of Usmanov's actions pleased Jack; it was the reason he came to Moscow in the first place, to live a miserable existence until his eventual self-inflicted death. In his lucid moments and also at his most ossified he pined for Aishling to be in his arms again, to be surrounded by her intoxicating aroma, the softness of her hair, her smooth cheek grazing against his stubble strewn face, to have one last embrace, to feel her soft smooth lips against his. He longed to talk to his son, about anything, about everything; about schools, the Jets' chances this year. Just to see him smile and be happy again. In his lucid moments he tried to block out such thoughts. In his drunkest it only made him down more Vodka – harder, faster and stronger.

5,7" Marat Usmanov was fat. He bordered on obese. He had huge jowls and his neck had not been a visible singular entity for many years. His belly was so bulbous, Jack often wondered whether he had to ask people whether his shoe laces were tied or not. He had massively podgy stubs of fingers. He was bald on the top of his head yet every hair at the sides was treated with great care and attention. He wore gold rimmed reading glasses which constantly resided at the bottom of his nose.

Jack's partner Mostovoi did his best to look out for him particularly when he could sense an impending Usmanov attack on the horizon. He did his utmost to keep Jack out of his path; asking him to go to research something in the archives or question a suspect on the other side of the building, bringing him out of the office for lunch, anything that would keep him out of Usmanov's path.

Twenty nine year old Mostovoi had been married for two years to his wife Dasha. They had a new born son

Rafis who was their pride and joy. 5'11" with thick black straight hair which drooped over his ears, he was a very promising young cop. Jack often thought to himself that he would have been proud to have him on his team back in New York; he felt lucky to have him as a partner now in Moscow.

Despite growing up the Russian community in Brighton Beach Jack had never warmed to Russian cuisine and as his mother and subsequently Aishling had always cooked for him he had never learned to cook and had no intention of learning now. Aishling frequently joked that he could 'burn water'. As such the only thing he ate for Lunch and Dinner was fast food – McDonalds, KFC, Burger King. He never ate breakfast due to the pounding headaches and sickly feeling in his stomach and mouth he would have from drinking heavily the night before. He frequently wondered to himself which might kill him first - the Vodka or the Big Macs.

Chapter 32

#59 – Monika Onatop reverently lit a candle and knelt in front of the 18th century icon, which observed her piously from on high, in front of her. She prayed for her family back in Ukraine and that tonight would be a good night; with nice customers. When she had finished, she got to her feet and made her way to the door of the tiny Russian Orthodox Church, one metro stop away from where she worked - the Bittsa Park metro station was her patch.

The Russian Orthodox Church is in communion with the other Eastern Orthodox Churches. The onion dome is typical of many Orthodox churches. Russian Orthodox Church buildings differ in design from many western-type churches. Most notably the interiors are enriched with many sacramental objects including holy icons, which hang on the walls. In addition, murals often cover most of the interior. Most of these images represent saints, and scenes from their lives.

Gold is the colour which resembles the Heavenly Kingdom. It is also used to add a sense of indefinite depth to icons, which would otherwise be perceived as flat. Painted icons are intentionally composed in a two-dimensional, non-perspective fashion to allow equal viewing regardless of the placement, position, and angle of the observing person, as well as to emphasize that the depiction is primarily of a spiritual truth rather than of visible reality.

In Russian Orthodox churches there are no pews. Most churches are lit with candles rather than electric light. Virtually all churches have multiple votive candle stands in front of the icons. It is customary for worshippers to purchase candles in church stores, light them, and place them on the stands. This ritual signifies a person's prayer to God, the Holy Mother, or to the saints or angels asking for help on the difficult path to salvation and to freedom from sin.

As she moved Monika tried in vain to lengthen her sequined mini skirt to cover up more of her legs than it usually did. Her three and a half inch white stiletto heels echoed throughout the deserted church, as she edged towards the door.

Outside the sun was setting,

which signified that it was time to go to work. Monika had been living in Moscow for a little over three years. She had moved from Kiev in Ukraine when she was nineteen with the hope that Moscow would be a city of opportunity for her. She struggled to get a job and as a Ukrainian in Russia suffered from discrimination when trying to apply for positions that she knew she would be perfect for. Monika did not want to go back to Ukraine as a failure – she had told all her friends and family how successful she was going to be when she moved to Moscow, how rich she was going to become. It was all she ever talked about in the months before she left for Moscow.

After six months, she had no job and no money and would have to come home ashamed if she did not manage to find work fast. She fell into prostitution entirely unintentionally; one night as she was waiting for a taxi on the street to go and meet some friends in a bar, a strange car pulled up and the driver propositioned her for sex – in exchange for money. She was shocked and horrified at such a depraved suggestion and refused point blank. The driver of the car sped away apologetically. As the days and nights passed she could not get her mind off the man's offer. She could do it, just for a short time – just while she was looking for a job and as soon as she found one she would quit immediately. Now, two and a half years later she had still not been able to quit – she needed the money. She worked all night, slept most of the day and as such never had time to look for a job. Also her early rejections when trying to find a job had knocked her confidence and she could not take the rejection again. At least in her current job she was in demand – wanted, desired and in control. It gave her a slight sense of power that she had not felt in those helpless days she spent fruitlessly looking for a job and being dismissed out of hand – not because of her abilities but because of where she came from.

She told her friends and parents that she was working in a luxurious office in Moscow's business district (Moscow International Business Centre, nicknamed Moskva City) – that she was working for a millionaire, of which there were many in Moscow. She told them that she worked as his personal assistant, that the job was very glamorous and paid good money. The reality, unfortunately for her, was very different. In order to justify her lie she would send home money every month. This would leave her with just enough to get by every month; pay the rent and buy groceries. No money for things like new furniture or the latest fashions – things that most girls her age were buying without giving a second thought to.

As she stepped off the metro in Bittsa Park metro station her high heels announced her arrival on the granite floor. The station features two rows of twenty six deep pink marble columns. It also features grey granite floor and dark green track walls faced with ornamental metal panels. As well as her white stiletto heels and black sequined mini skirt she was wearing black fish net stockings, a red boob tube and a black mac which she left open so as not to conceal her assets to potential customers.

5,3", with a slim figure Monika had shoulder length red hair. She dyed it herself and it was obvious she had. When she was working she wore heavy make-up; red lipstick, thick foundation, eyeliner, mascara and colourful eye shadow. When she was not working she never wore any make up. She looked far better that way. She noticed the heavy make-up was damaging her otherwise healthy, youthful skin. But the make-up attracted the customers so she had to wear it to make money.

One of her front teeth slightly overlapped the other. She was very conscious of it and always did her best to hide it, often covering her month when she spoke. Yet many of her customers commented on how cute it was and that she had lovely teeth. She did, but such kind comments did little to alleviate her complex.

Chikalito had been cogently encouraging Joseph to kill a prostitute for some time now until finally he relented. From frequenting Bittsa Park on so many occasions Joseph knew that many 'worked' the area and the adjacent metro station.

Joseph approached Monika as she stood looking off into space disinterested in life. She was standing in her patch; behind the metro station. The only people who came around there were people making deliveries and people looking for her to have sex. Frequently the former became the latter.

As she heard someone approaching she sprang into life and into 'work mode'. "Hey baby" she said to

Joseph "...wanna screw?" She had overheard other girls saying this line when she first started working the night and she had said it ever since. Most of her customers loved it when she said it. But it was so against her nature to say such a thing that every time she said it she felt a twinge of anxiety in her stomach; like it chipped away a piece of her soul.

"Eh yeah, yes... I do" She could see by Joseph's awkward response and his general demeanour that the 'full on' approach, which her other customers loved, was making him uncomfortable so she decided to tone it down a little.
- "You wanna go somewhere to be with me baby?"
- "Yeah, yes. How about across the road to Bittsa Park, somewhere quiet?"
- "Ok sweetie, whatever you say".

As they made their way through Bittsa Park it was starting to get dark, it was just past 9:30 pm on a Wednesday night in the middle of July.

Joseph took her to one of his usual spots, a place where he would usually kill one of the homeless drunks that called the park home. He started talking about Dragan; a usual ploy to lull his victims into a false sense of security. But this time the person hearing the story was not getting ever more inebriated by drinking from a bottle of Vodka. Monika was working and was there to perform a service and leave, not waste time talking – much less reminiscing about a dog.

"Slice off her nipples" Chikalito trumpeted in. "Do it and we will eat them later, cook them and eat them". Joseph did his best to ignore him. Monika needed to hurry this job up and get back to her patch for the opportunity to make more money. Being a prostitute was all about volume and she knew it.

"You seem stressed" she said getting up off the park bench where they sat in a secluded part of the park. "Why not let me try and relax you?" Joseph did not know what to say – this was not part of the plan for how he was going to kill her. She knelt down in front of him unzipped his pants and started to masturbate Joseph until he became hard. He quickly did. Then she started to perform fallacio on him. Joseph did not know what to do or where to look. He looked at Chikalito for guidance – "Kill her" he mouthed.

Joseph did not derive sexual pleasure from killing like Chikalito did. In fact Joseph had never been sexually aroused before in his life. A fact he increasingly justified to himself as proof that he was above other humans and in fact a god. Why would a god be aroused by vermin? was how he rationalised it to himself. The only love he had ever felt was for his mother and his dogs.

With his penis in her mouth, Monika stared up at Joseph whilst she continued to perform the sex act on him. As soon as Joseph made eye contact with Monika, coupled with the action she was performing on him and his penis – a euphoric ecstasy washed over him and enraptured him and his entire body. He had never felt such a sensation before. He had ejaculated. He was unsure what had just happened. About what he was feeling? As Monika rose from her knees to sit beside him, Joseph sat on the park bench in the deserted area of Bittsa Park in a state of shock. When Monika saw this she put it down to her great performance and looked off into the empty woods to her right satisfied with herself and with the power she held over men. How much would she charge for such a performance? was her next thought.

Despite the immediate elation Joseph felt he now sat there completely dejected. How could a god allow an insect to pleasure him like this? How could he really be a god and above humans if he found satisfaction in what she did to him? Almost as if Chikalito had sensed Joseph's current state of mind he came behind him and whispered in his ear "Kill her, Kill the bitch, she is dirt!"

Suddenly Joseph's dejection ascended into a blind fit of rage. Without a moment's hesitation to pull up his trousers he rose up whilst pulling his hammer from his inside jacket pocket and as Monika was turning around to request due payment for her services he smashed her on the left side of the head with the hammer. There was so much force and hatred in that one blow Joseph managed to knock Monika clean off the park bench she had been sitting on. By the time her body hit the ground she was already dead. One quick look and Joseph could see that square fifty nine was ready to be branded with an x.

"Slice her nipples off" Chikalito

excitedly yelled out to the deserted park. Joseph pulled his pants up and looked at Chikalito. He did not want to do such a thing. He would not derive the same, or any, pleasure as Chikilito would from doing so. "We will cook them later". Joseph was at pains to say it but he forced himself to say "No!". "No I will not do it" he said. Chikalito's sickening grin vanished. Joseph knew he would have to do something to appease his brother, friend and mentor. Especially after refusing to cut off Timur's testicles as a present for him.

He lent over Monika's body, placed her on her back, withdrew a switch blade from his back pocket and with a final look of desperation at Chikalito – whose face was now a picture of excitement as what he was seeing before his eyes, Joseph sliced off Monika's plum cheeks and put them into the sports bag he had brought with him that lay on the ground beside the park bench. "Yes, yes wait till you see my brother. They will be so tasty. Not as good as nipples and no comparison to young boys testicles but good none the less".

Joseph shrugged and feigned a

weak smile at Chikalito, hoping he would stop talking about the vile subject. He was certainly not looking forward to the prospect of eating another human beings cheeks, or any part of a human for that matter. He knew he would not enjoy the experience but Chikalito was practically euphoric about it and could not wait to get home and start cooking Monika's cheeks.

As they exited the park they were shocked to see a police car at the gates. When they looked over at the Metro station they could see there were two police men stopping people as they went in and out of the station.

They had already made eye contact with one of the officers, so making a run for it in order to avoid being questioned was now out of the question. The policeman who had made eye contact with Joseph stopped him as he approached the station. He asked him had he seem anything or anyone unusual in the area recently as they were searching for a killer who had possibly escaped from the mental hospital in the park. Joseph informed the officer that he had seen nothing. When asked what was in the bag? Chikalito chuckled and said "the plump juicy cheeks of a prostitute we just killed, we are going to eat them when we get home". Joseph nudged him to shut up. The police officer wondered why Joseph had made such an odd movement with his left arm but he put it down to an involuntary tick. "Oh nothing, I was looking for wild mushrooms in the park but could not find any good ones, so have given up looking for the night" Joseph said to the questioning policeman. The officer took Joseph's details and allowed him to go on his way.

Chapter 33

Tvoi Dyen

Bittsa Park Maniac terrorises city
Yvengani Stankovic reporting

The 18th corpse, that of a so far unidentified young woman, was found on Wednesday. Police are pursuing the possibility that the woman may have been a prostitute who worked in the area. She had been battered on the head with a heavy object. Police say that at least nine of the 18 murders that have occurred in the park are the work of the 'maniac'. The others are believed to be the work of different killers though police cannot be sure. With one exception, all of the murders have taken place in the northern half of the park. The 'maniac' follows a well-established pattern – until now his or her victims were all men aged between fifty and seventy and were all killed by a blow to the back of the head with a heavy object. The killer always strikes in the evening or at night and does not kill for financial gain, never taking the victim's money or documents. The men killed so far were poor pensioners and mostly homeless people. Though the latest victim is a woman, almost all of the other victims were male and psychologists have speculated that 'the Maniac' may hold a grudge against men. Police believe the killer befriends his or her victims by offering them alcohol, the consumption of which is common in Moscow parks.

Muscovites have their own theory about the killings. They suspect the murderer is a patient from the hospital for the psychologically disturbed which is located in the park close to the spot where most of the bodies were found.

The hospital admits it allows some of its more stable patients to stroll in the park and says it cannot rule out the possibility one of them might be the murderer. "Our patients are like children", the hospital's director, told this reporter "We let the stable one walk in the park, the others we don't. But anything could happen. They run off sometimes and climb over the fence". "The Maniac" is described as being powerfully built, though police appear to have little idea of what they are dealing with and have not ruled out the possibility the murderer could even be a woman. Twice the police have detained (and in one case shot) suspects only to have to let them go for lack of evidence. The first pulled a knife on them when confronted and ran off – he later explained he thought the police were trying to mug him. The second turned out to be a cross-dressing transvestite who had a hammer in their handbag. Police though they had their man. But the transvestite turned out to have a solid alibi for all the murders and was released.

The killings have frightened local residents. "We don't want to live here anymore," said one. "This place is somehow cursed. How many more bodies are they going to find here?" The police have set up a task force to catch the killer and have assigned plain-clothes policemen to patrol the park. Anxious to allay local fears, the authorities have promised to build a police station in the park, to erect fencing around its perimeter, to install CCTV cameras, and to put in street lamps along its walkways.

Chapter 34

Some days later there was a knock on Joseph's apartment door. It was the police. They brought him in for questioning as he had been seen leaving the park the night a prostitute had been killed. They had found semen in the victim's mouth. Semen of the killer it was safe to assume.

The officer who questioned Joseph was Jack Wolfe's partner in the Muscovite police force Pavel Mostovoi. He was convinced Joseph was the person who killed the prostitute Monika Onatop and maybe even the person who had killed the other victims they suspected 'the Bittsa Park Maniac' of killing.

Mostovoi would have loved Jacks help questioning Joseph but unfortunately for him, during the short period of a few days that they held Joseph in jail under suspicion of killing Monika Onatop, Jack was worse than Mostovoi had ever seen him; sometimes not even coming work and when he did he was completely drunk, depressed and utterly unable to contribute in any meaningful way to the case in hand. It was all Mostovoi could do to keep Jack out of

Usmanov's warpath during this time. All in all, he was quite annoyed with Jack: they were so close to cracking a crucial case yet he was merely a shell of a man at this pivotal time. Yet as much as Jack's behaviour was growing tiresome, Mostovoi was more concerned than anything else for the wellbeing of his partner – a man he liked to think of as a friend. Why was he doing this to himself? and why was had there been such a dramatic deterioration in him now?

Little was Mostovoi to know, and unfortunately for all concerned, the very time the police had Joseph locked up on suspicion of being 'the Bittsa Park Maniac' was also the anniversary of Jack's beloved wife Ashling's slaying at the clutches of 'Bigfoot', as such, during this time Jack was morbidly depressed and also brilliantly belligerent. Mostovoi made sure to keep him down in the records department, out of Usmanov's gaze, when he turned up to work during this time. When he did not even bother to turn up, he pretended that Jack was out chasing a lead critical to crack the case.

Mostovoi had an unerring suspicion he could not shake off that the upper echelons of the police force were not overly concerned with catching 'the Bittsa Park Maniac'. He tried to stop himself from thinking such thoughts but he could not help feel that whilst the 'Maniac' was killing homeless drunks and prostitutes in a rundown area of Moscow, far away from the glamour and riches of Moscow city centre the 'powers that be' of the Muscovite police were not going to over exert themselves trying to catch him or devote significant man power to the task. Nevertheless Mostovoi was determined to get one more killer off the streets, regardless of who he was killing and all the evidence was pointing to Joseph being the killer of Monika Onatop.

The police took his blood and were sure they had the person who committed the crime. They were sure they had found their man, 'the Bittsa Park Maniac', but when they got the results back from the laboratory they were shocked. The blood sample they took from Joseph did not match that of the person who secreted the semen into Monika Onatop's mouth. Mostovoi was devastated. As there was no match and no more evidence against Joseph they were forced to let him go.

Even Joseph was surprised that he was not charged with the crime. His heart sank when they told him the killer's semen was found in the victim's mouth. He had forgotten all about that and was sure the game was up, over before he would have a chance to finish his masterpiece. Fortunately for him yet unfortunately for Mostovoi, Joseph was a chimera. In Greek mythology a chimera was an animal with the head of a lion, the body of a goat and the tail of a dragon; a genetic anomaly. These genetic anomalies exist in nature today and also in human beings (less than one hundred cases have been reported) whereby one person can have two entirely different sets of DNA and as such, as in Joseph case, a person's semen will not necessarily match their blood type. He had been very lucky, the police had come tantalisingly close to catching him but they were unsuccessful and he was still on course to achieving his masterpiece.

Chapter 35

"Hey dude, wake up", "*Bordel de Merde!* - wake the hell up man". It was 6:20 am and Jean Paul had been trying to wake Luke up for the last five minutes to no avail and time was increasingly becoming more of the issue. Jean Paul felt Luke was leaving him with no other choice, in order to wake him up drastic measures were required - 'a nipple twister'!. Luke was laying on his back snoring the apartment down, so performing the act would be relatively easy. He grabbed Luke's nipple between his thumb and index finger and twisted as if he was trying to open a bottle top.

Instantaneously the room was filled with a long drawn out scream from Luke. "Get the hell off me man" he yelled, "What?" "What do you want?" he begged agitatedly. "Wake up asshole" Jean Paul said with a smile "we're going to Russia today... to get wrecked!" his voice rising at the end of the sentence for comic effect. "Ewh" Luke said in disgust as he rolled over and plunged his face into his pillow "I can't be bothered going" he was serious; his bed was probably the most comfortable it had been since he moved into the apartment.

"If you don't get up in the next five minutes I will leave without you...". That one comment was better than any alarm clock; the idea of Jean Paul on the vodka trail having a great time without him, made Luke suddenly wake up.

"I'm up, I'm up, jeez" Luke said. He sat on his bed eyes closed in a semi-comatose state. He was so tired. With one eye half open he looked at the time on his digital clock radio, "6:24 am – this is inhuman". He got to his feet and started to get changed – all with only one eye half open, this way according to his logic, it went someway to still being asleep.

After a quick bite to eat they left their apartment and got a taxi to the bus station. At 7:30 am they took the bus to Madrid, there they were greeted by gleeful taxi drivers eager to rip them off and overcharge them because they were not Spanish. They did not have time to figure out how to get a bus or a train to the airport so were forced to get a taxi. They were easily recognisable as tourists and as such were duly swindled by their sullen taxi driver. €43 for a fifteen minute journey, they considered not paying but knew they had little choice. Two hours later they boarded their plane and commenced the five hour trip from Madrid to Moscow. They arrived at 11:30 pm local time – exhausted but happy to have finally arrived.

On the plane Jean Paul had regaled Luke with information about Moscow from his Russia Travel guide. Luke was quite happy to be informed of the highlights; it was a quick way of learning about their next destination without actually having to study anything about it.

"Moscow has been the Russian capital for over 850 years". "With a population of 8,300,000 Moscow is one of Europe's most populace cities. The currency in Russia is the Ruble (R)". Jean Paul quoted from his travel bible.

"Moscow's climate really consists of two seasons, -30 Degrees Celsius in the Winter and +30 Degrees Celsius in the Summer. Whilst we will be there Moscow will just have entered the period known as 'The Great Thaw' – this is when there is no snow anymore and it is a lot less cold than in the winter but it can rain heavily quite a lot"

"Check this out man" Jean Paul

said excitedly reading from the guide, finger underlining every word "Moscow is currently enjoying a period of unprecedented growth. It has one of the world's highest concentrations of billionaires. Twenty six of Russia's Thirty three billionaires live in the city. Much of this wealth has come from the country's rich natural resources- oil and gas. This has led to unrivalled levels of gentrification in Moscow city centre".

"Although there is great wealth Moscow's average salary is still relatively low compared to other European capitals and poverty becomes more obvious just a short distance from the city centre.

"Moscow was recently named the world's most expensive city! Moscow is the spiritual, political and economic capital of the World's largest country".

"The centre of the city is roughly formed by the garden ring. Most businesses, restaurants, shopping and entertainment centres are located within the garden ring".

"Moscow municipal transport: a well-developed net of metro, bus, and tram lines makes any area of the city accessible without having a car".

In Domodedovo airport, which is located twenty four miles south of the city centre, after several minutes looking around for an ATM they eventually fell upon a bankomat machine.

They withdrew the equivalent of €200 in roubles each and headed for the exit. By now it was close to midnight and neither were in any mood of trying to figure whether a bus or metro system would take them where they needed to go. There was a queue of taxis waiting outside the airport. They made their way towards them. Jean Paul had his Russia travel guide in his left hand; he had bought it especially for the trip he managed to come across an English version in *El Corte Ingles* which was only a two minute walk from where their apartment was located in Granada.

They walked right up to the first taxi driver in the queue, a slender stoic man with dark eyes and stubble on his face. Jean Paul opened up his guide to the part relating to accommodation in Moscow, he pointed to one, the taxi driver nodded without saying a word. Jean Paul and Luke looked at each other with a momentary rush of uncertainty, they soon realised they had little choice but to proceed, they both shrugged, put their luggage in the boot of the car and got in the back.

Whilst driving into the city centre Luke turned to Jean Paul "So what is the name of the place we are staying again?" Reading from the page relating to hotels and hostels in his guide he said "It's called... The Europa Hotel". "Europa Hotel" Luke repeated aloud as they drove closer towards the neon colossus that represents the beating heart of Russia. Luke was useless when it came to organising such things; he had left all the arrangements for the trip – flights, hotels, train tickets up to Jean Paul. All Luke had to do was simply supply his credit card at the appropriate moment when Jean Paul was booking anything for the trip. Jean Paul did not mind, he quite liked the responsibility of organising all the elements of a trip like this.

"Yes, it's right in the centre of the city, and it's cheap! We are there for three nights, tonight included and then we get the Vodka train to its first destination on the Journey – St Petersburg".
Luke lay his head against the car window

as it sped along hoping to catch a few moments sleep. Without paying Luke any notice Jean Paul started to read aloud from the travel guide sections on Moscow again.

The taxi driver looked into his rear view mirror at Jean Paul whilst he read aloud. Raising his eyebrows momentarily and shaking his head more in wonder than amusement. "these guys will not last five minutes in this city".

As a native Muscovite, born and bred he was more than aware of how increasingly dangerous Moscow was becoming, not to mention the city's latest scourge – 'the Bittsa Park Maniac' but he figured as tourists they would have little reason to venture so far away from the city centre and as such they would surely not have any reason to cross the killer's path.

After a fifty minute journey they eventually pulled up to their hostel. Their taxi cost 930 roubles, around €50 Jean Paul was not sure whether they being ripped off or whether this the normal price as he knew Moscow was one the most expensive cities in the world.

A one metre long building was wedged in

between a convenience store on one side and a bar on the other. Both were closed. The blue door that was the entrance to the hotel was also closed. Above the door a blue neon sign confirmed they were in the right place. In cursive it spelt 'Europa Hotel'.

"There will be a night porter or something" Luke said to Jean Paul as he pressed the buzzer and simultaneously their taxi driver sped off into the night. No answer. Luke pressed it again, once he and Jean Paul had exchanged a look to confirm that it was the right thing to do. After what felt like an eternity, much to their delight, there was a response "*Dah?*". Jean Paul moved towards the intercom "Yes... hi, we... we have a reservation, two beds... for three nights" After a full minute a response came "name?" demanded the intercom in a thick Russian accent. "Cigcen" came Jean Paul's repost in an equally thick French accent, his mouth right up at the intercom. Again they waited and waited until finally the door buzzed and allowed them to enter.

They opened the door and were immediately greeted by a narrow flight of stairs. They tentatively made their way up the stairs in single file as only one person could fit at a time and with their rucksacks on their backs even that was a struggle. The top of the stairs opened out into the foyer of the hotel. It was surprisingly large considering the size of the stairs they had just come up. The hostel clearly operated above the convenience store and bar that flanked it, which Jean Paul and Luke had noticed when they got out of the taxi. Directly in front of them was a hallway which they could see led off to the hostel rooms. To their right was a communal area for people to sit and chat or watch TV and behind that was the reception. Sitting at the reception desk in the unlit room, darkness only interrupted by a solitary desk lap, was a shadowy, stocky figure. They made their way towards him. "Hi… we have a room booked, for three nights, Cigcen is the name" Jean Paul said. The figure did not move. They watched him as they moved toward the desk. He never once budged, just stared at them in a manner that unnerved the two.

Then, without warning, as if he had just awoken from a paralysing trance, he arose from his seat "follow" he said as he came from behind the desk and led them in the direction of the rooms. Jean

Paul and Luke looked at each other for a moment, unsure whether to follow this strange person or not. Tiredness over took Luke and he began to follow the night porter.

When they found the night porter he was waiting outside of a room, room number six, with the door open. "This is room", he said. "Ok great" Jean Paul said as they made their way past him into the room. It was empty except for four bunk beds. 'we are the only ones in the room…sweet' Luke thought to himself. Jean Paul dropped his bag on the floor and went back to the door were the night porter was still standing. "Thank you for all your help" he said holding out his hand "I'm Jean Paul and he is Luke" he said as he shook the night porters hand. He looked disinterested. He began to leave. "And what is your name?" Jean Paul begged. The night porter turned and manically looked Jean Paul in the eye "Joseph" the night porter said "Joseph, Joseph…great! nice to meet you Joseph" Jean Paul said with a smile. With that Joseph left them and returned to his post.

"Seems like a bit of an oddball!" Luke said to Jean Paul once the door was closed. "No, they all just seem like that at first, sullen, stoic, menacing… just give them a chance and you will see they are fine". "Yeah suppose so" Luke said. He was too tired to have a debate about it. He went straight to bed.

Chapter 36

By the time Jean Paul woke up, 9:37am the next morning, Luke had already been awake for over an hour. Luke was not much of a night owl (unless there was alcohol involved, then he would be the last to go to bed) otherwise he would usually crash around 11:30 pm or 12:00 am as he had last night. With all the travelling yesterday and being up so early it was a long day but now he felt fully rested, recharged and ready for a new day and the adventure of seeing the wonders of Moscow which lay before them. He willed Jean Paul to wake up so they could begin.

As the minutes progressed with agonising sluggishness, Luke's mind began to wander. For the first time in a long time he allowed himself to wonder about his father. He had not spoken to him in over a year and a half and his heart was full to the brim with malice towards him. He was glad that they had chosen to come on the Vodka Trail, particularly instead of heading to Amsterdam and all that would have inevitably entailed. Equally he was exited that he would be getting to check out Moscow whilst he was here. He was curious to see what the 'commies', as his grandfather back in North Carolina would call them, were like. His only irrational worry was somehow running into his father in the short time he and Jean Paul were in the city "impossible!" - the word thrust forth out of his mouth like an truculent volcano.

He had not intended to speak aloud but his emotions had gotten the better of him. Luke quickly confirmed that he had not unintentionally woken up his friend and roommate. He had not. Jean Paul was still sound asleep 'god he could sleep through a hurricane' he whispered to himself. It was notoriously easy for Jean Paul to fall asleep and stay that way regardless of where he was – in a plane, a bus, someone else's apartment or even a hostel room in Moscow, Luke and the others often joked with him about it.

He knew, as his grandparents tried, whenever possible to broach the subject of his estranged father with him, that his father was working for the muscovite police force but other than that he did not know anything about what his father's life now involved in Moscow. He did not want to know either. Much to his immediate regret, Luke had mentioned some months ago to Jean Paul, long before the possibility of travelling to Moscow had ever been discussed, that he had a father who worked in Moscow as a cop. He told him that they no longer spoke. That was all he gave up and Jean Paul did not pursue the matter further scavenging for further detail, figuring if Luke wanted to reveal more he would do so in his own time. It was after they had all been out at club Camborio one Friday night, the others had gone to sleep and in a sublimely inebriated state he allowed his guard to slip regarding his father's existence. Jean Paul never brought up the subject again and Luke hoped he wouldn't over the next few days whilst they were in Moscow.

"Hey man" Luke said as Jean Paul yawned loudly, announcing to the empty room he was awake. Sitting up and looking half eyed at Luke he nodded good morning to his friend. "Sleep well?" Luke ventured. Accompanied by an equally vigorous yawn as the first, Jean Paul said "Yes, you?"

-" Yeah not bad! So what's on the agenda for today?"
- "First shower, then eat, then check out

all this city has to offer" Ok? Is that cool with you?" Jean Paul said.
- "Yeah man, sounds great!"

As they were leaving the hotel around 10:15 am Luke noticed a poster in the lobby.
- "Hey man, check this out!" he said pointing to his proud discovery.
- "What?" Jean Paul lethargically responded still easing himself into the day.
- "Look, Dynamo Moscow are playing Spartak Moscow tonight. It is at the Luzniky Stadium. Match starts at 9:00pm and the best part – they are selling tickets for the game here at the reception desk. Six hundred roubles. How much is that is euros?"

Eyes now lit up with excitement Jean Paul earnestly responded "€35 euros a ticket". "What do you think? Would you be interested?" Luke tentatively foraged. "Yes, that would be great to go to that, see some Russian football, that would be really cool!"

After a not too significant amount of pointing and money waving they managed to successfully buy tickets for the match. *"Spasibo, Spasibo, Do*

Svidanaya" Jean Paul said gleefully pocketing the tickets all the while reading, in a very heavy French accent, from his travel guide.

As they walked out of the hostel and onto the street Luke nudged Jean Paul "Yo man, what did you say to that girl at reception?" "Nothing much, I just said thank you and good bye, when you fell asleep last night I read the section in my travel guide relating to Russian vocabulary". "That's cool man! So where are we off to first?" "I need something to eat. I am really hungry!". "Yeah no sweat, guess we will just find somewhere along here" Luke said referring to the street which Hotel Europa was located. "What is the name of this street again?" he asked. "Plotnikov Pereulok" Jean Paul replied reading from the map in his guide book. "*Pereulok*' means lane. Actually I read in the book last night that '*Ulitsa*' is street, '*Prospekt*' is avenue, '*Ploshchad*' is square, '*Bulvar*' is boulevard and '*Most*' means bridge. In fact there is a really great restaurant in the city centre called 'Most' but it's too expensive for us to check out'.

"Huh, that's funny. Thank god you got that book before we left, otherwise we'd be totally screwed and completely lost in this place". Luke said.

It did not take long to find somewhere to have breakfast. As they took their seats in the empty and otherwise non-descript café they were promptly handed the '*Zautrak*' (the menu). Luke was not one to eat much for breakfast whereas Jean Paul would eat anything, anytime. Jean Paul went from the guide book to the menu and back again searching for some words, any words he recognised. Eventually he came across something that was also in the guide book.

"Hey they have fried eggs, see '*Yoichnitsa*', would you eat that? he asked Luke. "Yeah sure, why not, may as well eat something". When the po faced waitress eventually sauntered over to them Jean Paul ordered 'Two (holding up two fingers, indicating the order was to be doubled for both he and Luke) *yoichnitsa* and *kleb* and *koffe*"

Luke looked confused, picking up on this Jean Paul offered "I just ordered some bread and coffee also". As Luke did not drink coffee he queried "Do they have anything else to drink?" His friend handed him the guide open on the 'Eating Out' section. Quickly scanning the open page the only other beverage he could find was milk "*Moloko* please" he sheepishly said to the un-amused waitress. "*Dah*" Jean Paul said taking the book back from his friend and summarised their order "one *Koffe* (putting up one finger), one *moloko*, two *yoichnitsa* and two *kleb. Spasibo*".

The food, when it eventually arrived, was ok. Luke would have killed for some ketchup to put on his fried eggs but the word was not in the travel guide. At least he managed to get some '*perets*' (pepper) and '*sol*' (salt) which greatly helped instil a modicum of flavour into his otherwise lifeless eggs and the '*maslo*' (butter) for his bread worked wonders.

- "So where we off to first?" Luke ask
- "Red square" Jean Paul replied excitedly consulting his travel guide.
- "Cool!"
- "There we can see the Kremlin and Saint Peters Basilica. What do you think?"
- "Sounds like a plan".
- "After lunch I was thinking we might go to the *banyas*".

- "What are '*banyas*'?"
- "They are these great traditional bath houses they have over here, you steam yourself in a crazy hot steam room, then you cool down in an ice-cool pool, then you do it all over again. You can drink beer – it is very typically Russian. What to you think?
- "Sounds awesome dude!"
- "Sweet, if we have enough time today we will do that".
- "Well what are we waiting for lets get this show on the road".
- "Cool lets go".

They paid the bill and left. They walked along Gagarinsky Pereulok until it intersected with Gogolorusky Bulvar. On their right was the Kropotkinskaya metro stop. "So what line do we need to take?" Luke asked Jean Paul as he looked at the map of the Moscow metro system which looked more like a child's drawing of an alien space craft than anything else; multiple colourful lines emanating outwards and intersecting a brown circle.

"We need to take the red line two stops until we reach Okhotny Ryad, there we can walk to Red Square". "How much is it?" Luke asked his friend as they neared the ticket office. "It's around seventeen roubles – less than one euro". "Sweet!". Having purchased their tickets and waiting on the platform for the train to arrive Jean Paul turned to Luke "Hey you see that?" "What?" "That!" Jean Paul repeated pointing to the brown circular line which joined all the other lines on the metro map. "Yeah? What's up?" "I read the other day in my guide that there is an urban legend about the origin of the ring line of the Moscow Metro. They say a group of engineers approached Stalin with plans for the Metro, to inform him of the current progress of the project. As he looked at the drawings, Stalin poured himself some coffee and spilt a small amount over the edge of the cup. When he was asked whether or not he liked the project so far, he put his cup down on the centre of the Metro blueprints and left in silence. The bottom of the cup left a brown circle on the drawing. The planners looked at it and realized that it was exactly what they had been missing. Taking it as a sign of Stalin's genius, they gave orders for the building of the ring line that connected all the other lines, which on metro maps is always printed in brown!"

"Huh, that is a wild story! Especially if it is true! So where is the board to show when the next train is coming? Luke questioned. "There is no time table or board to show when the next train is coming. I read in the book that the metro system in Moscow is the largest and most efficient in the world, seven million people a day use it. During peak times trains run around every ninety seconds on most lines.

"Whoa!, that is crazy – 'most efficient in the world?' Luke repeated incredulously "better that New York, London, Paris or Tokyo?" he queried. "Well that is what the book says man" Jean Paul replied. "Huh" was all Luke could muster as he shrugged his shoulders.

Suddenly there was a flurry of activity. The train was coming. Promptly announcing its glorious arrival the tanoy proclaimed the event. As they stepped onto the train Jean Paul turned to Luke and said "You hear that?" "What, the announcer? Luke asked looking at his friend perplexed "don't tell me you understood what it said?".

"No, not necessarily" Jean Paul said as he opened his travel guide and started reading aloud. Before he begun he looked up at his friend and confirmed "The announcer – that was a male announcer right?" "Eh yeah" Luke replied, still confused. Jean Paul read aloud 'On all lines travellers can determine the direction of the train by the gender of the announcer: on the radial lines, travellers heading toward the centre of Moscow will hear male-voiced announcements, and travellers heading away will hear female-voiced announcements (a good rule is: 'your boss calls you to work; your wife calls you home').

"I like it man, that is cool thing to remember" Luke said, marvelling at how much his friend already knew about the city they were about to explore.

As they entered Resurrection gate, the main entrance into Red Square, they passed 'Kilometre zero' marked on the pavement in front of them: the point where all distances in Russia were once measured from.

Directly in front of them as they passed through the gate was the fantasy castle-esque structure (which would not be out of place in a Disney movie) that is Saint Basil's Basilica, some seven hundred meters a head of them. In Red Square itself, on the right was the Kremlin: the spiritual, artistic and ruling heart of Russia, a sixty eight acre triangle of land overlooking the serpentine Moskva River which slithers its way through the centre of the city.

Moscow itself retains the basic layout of any Russian city; a Kremlin (fortress) in the centre surrounded by a series of concentric ring roads, with the main thoroughfares out of the city like spokes in a wheel.

Directly opposite the Kremlin is the leviathan that is GUM, the state department store. Strolling in the general direction of the Kremlin Luke asked Jean Paul "Hey dude, you think we might be able to check out Lenin's body?" "Don't know, let me see" Jean Paul replied consulting their tour guide, the travel book. "Well its open Wednesday, Thursday, Saturday and Sunday between 10:00 am and 1:00 pm. What time is it now? (looking at his watch he answered his own question) 12:10 pm, you want to check it out?" "Yeah, sure why not? Could be pretty cool and I bet my grandfather would get a kick out of it. Might be cutting it a little fine though. I would imagine there is a pretty big line, especially with it being Saturday and all".

"Sure let's go see in anyway, besides it's free entry!" Jean Paul said. "Even better let's go" replied Luke. After waiting for thirty five minutes they entered the darkened room where Lenin's body lay. Several minutes later they emerged to the chilly, overcast Moscow weather thoroughly underwhelmed by the macabre and peculiar experience. "I bet the father of Communism and the founder of the Soviet Union would abhor the idea of his body being on display for tourists like us to gawk at" Jean Paul said. "Totally man, I completely agree it is a little sick, well at least we can say we did it'.

Given the significant entrance fee and equally significant queues to enter Saint Basils Basilica – so named after the barefoot holy man Vasil (Basil) who correctly predicted the downfall of Ivan the terrible, they decided not to go inside. Instead they opted to take a plethora of pictures of themselves standing outside the edifice and of its iconic multi-coloured domes.

"Hey you want to check out this

GUM place, see is there anything worth buying then go get something to eat?" Jean Paul asked his friend. "Sounds like a plan buddy" Luke replied. They walked around the wonderfully airy department store and each bought a bottle of Russian Vodka in the super market Sedmoy Kontinent. "This baby is for the train to Saint Petersburg, the first leg of the Vodka Trail, on Monday morning". Luke said to Jean Paul proudly placing his bottle of vodka into his rucksack like a father placing his first born into its cot, as they found themselves back in Red Square.

"So where to now man?" Luke asked. "Well i see in the book that we are not too far from a restaurant called 'Mayak'. It's located in the Mayakovskiy theatre. It is on Bolshaya Nikitskaya Ulitsa, around a fifteen minute walk west from here, what do you think?"

"Let's go man, I'm starving" Luke said already heading for resurrection gate. It ended up being more like thirty minutes before they managed to find the restaurant but when they did they were pleasantly surprised, great food at a reasonable price, particularly for Moscow. The theatrical décor merely added to the experience. The place had a nice mix of Russians and foreigners so it was not too over whelming for them yet not too 'touristy'. The smoky atmosphere suited Jean Paul but less so Luke who hated smoke but even he had to admit it accentuated the atmosphere of the place so he did his best not to let it bother him.

They both ordered 'Salad Oliver' – a salad made of potato, onions, pickles and thin strips or chicken and beef, dressed with mayonnaise. When ordering Jean Paul turned to the waiter and instructed "*Bez smetany*", "*Bez ukropa*" to which the pleasant garcon nodded dutifully.

"Hey what the hell did you just say to him? Luke asked confounded at his friends ability to grasp so much of the local language so quickly. "A lot of Russian dishes are served with lots of dill or sour cream, I just told him not to put any on our dishes". "Oh okay thanks man, god you must have studied that whole book before we came here!"

Shrugging his shoulders and protruding his bottom lip in a quintessentially Gallic manner Luke was suddenly reminded that despite his wonderful English Jean Paul was very much a French man. "No, I just read the important bits, things that I thought we might need". "Well I'm glad you did cause otherwise we would be lost" Luke said smiling to his friend. To accompany their *Zakushi* (salad course) they sipped chilled pepper and honey Vodka. "So what is next on the itinerary?" Luke asked.

"Well, we could go to the *banyas*, chill out for the afternoon, have a steam, drink a couple of beers, then get some dinner and then head to the match. It is all in the same general direction – kind of north of the city" Jean Paul said. "Sounds sick man, we have to do that" "Cool, drink up, lets pay the bill and get out of here", Jean Paul said downing the rest of his vodka.

They got the red line two stops to Tvetnoy Bulvar, there they found the Sanduny bath house. After putting their bags in the *Khranenie* (cloak room) and getting changed all they needed was a *Prostynya* (sheet), a *Polotenste* (a towel) and *Venik* (a bough of branches). Fully accessorised they entered the strictly gender segregated steam room. They felt a little out of place and self-conscious.

Like all *banya* novices they sat on the bottom bench where he heat is lowest. Picking up the *venik* Luke turned to his friend and asked "What the hell are we meant to do with this? "We hit ourselves with it" Jean Paul replied sincerely. "Yeah right, stop playing" Luke baulked. "Seriously, they say it improves your circulation and lets the blood flow around your body better, look check it out". Just then a local rose up and commenced the self-flagellation process.

"I aint doing that!" Luke turned to Jean Paul eyes pleading with his friend to be pardoned from such a ritual. "You'll be fine, it's all part of the experience. You want to go to the pool cool down a little?" "Yeah ok, I'm boiling here!"

Plunging into the ice cool pool (*basseyn*) they felt truly alive and delighted to be on this momentous trip together. As they staggered back to the changing room for a *pivo* (beer) one of the locals yelled at them "*S lyogkim Parom*". Momentarily startled Jean Paul eventually replied "Thank you, *spasibo, spasibo*" much to the delight of the locals. "What did he just say man?" Luke begged. "They have an expression in the bath houses 'hope your steam was easy'.

I assume that was what he said, I could not really hear him that well, I was still slightly dazed from the icy water in the pool. He either said that or that he likes my body and wants to take me out...?" Jean Paul said.

"Ha! Well let's hope for your sake man it is the first one!" Luke said laughing at his friend.

After repeating the process several times over the course of the evening they felt thoroughly relaxed and invigorated... and hungry. "So where we gonna eat? Luke asked Jean Paul knowing full well he would already have something in mind.

"The book really recommends 'City Grill', it's not too expensive, has a good mix of food and it is not far from here". "Sounds prefect" Luke said "Exactly what I am in the mood for right now".

They passed over Ulitsa Petrovka, through Stolehniknov Pereluk and up Tvershaya Ulitsa – the main road in and out of the city, strewn with shops, bars and restaurants. After a fifteen minute walk they arrived at the boldly

The Chessboard Killer

decorated restaurant. Promptly seated they were struck by the heavy grey walls, subdued lighting scheme and large windows with yellow bluish light. The window, which separated the kitchen from the main room, allowing them to view the food being prepared, added to the drama of their dining experience.

- "What you going to have dude?"
- "Kebab and French fries" Jean Paul replied.
- "Really, do they have that here?"
- "Yeah I'm in the mood for something simple right now".
- "Yeah good call actually man, can you order that for me too?"
- "Sure!"

When the waiter eventually got around to asking them for their order in the bustling restaurant Jean Paul ordered "*Shashlyk, Kartofel Fri* and *Pivo*", "Two" pointing to himself and Luke indicating the order was to be doubled "*Pozhaluysta (Please), Spasibo*". Luke repeated "*Spasibo*" to the waiter as he scurried away to the kitchen, having picked up that it was the word for 'Thank you' in Russian throughout the course of the day from listening to Jean Paul.

When the food arrived it was delicious and exactly was they needed. "So" Luke said as they ate "what do you think of the Russian *chicas*?"

- "Yeah good", Jean Paul just about managed to say as he chewed the mouthful of kebab he had just taken. When he had swallowed it he continued – "they are very different from women in Western Europe, they have a unique look that is unmistakable and very distinctive. They are hot as hell though that is for sure, certainly up to my standard he concluded with a smile. What to you think?"

- "Yeah, yeah I totally agree, very different from western European girls and girls back home in America but some of these are smokin'!" Luke said surveying his environs targeting every good looking female with his glare.

- "Yes we definitely made the right decision to come on this trip as opposed to going to Amsterdam" Jean Paul said.

- "Totally! So glad we came here and the best thing is this is only day one; we still have the whole Vodka Trail to do. That is going to be sick – we are going to get so messed up on that train man" Luke laughed.

- "Yes and today is not even over yet, we still have the match which starts at 9:00

pm. What time is it now?"
- "7:25 pm"
- "Cool, we will leave here around quarter to eight and be at the Luzniki stadium in plenty of time".
- "Can't wait to see a real Russian football match!" Luke replied.

It was a short walk to Belorusskaya metro station, two stops on the green line and they had arrived at the Luzniki stadium. They didn't fail to be impressed by the immense 55,000 thousand multi-coloured seated stadium. With a running track separating the seats from the pitch. At first Jean Paul felt as little removed from the action as he was used to the white hot atmosphere of French stadia where the fans and players are separated by mere feet. But all of that changed when the match commenced. They were behind the goal that Spartak were shooting into in the first half, facing their own fans who ceaselessly sang and danced in union for their team whilst taunting the Dynamo fans. They had never seen anything like it before.

"This is wild!" Luke shouted to Jean Paul. "Yes I know, it's great!" he replied. "Hey, you have any idea what they are saying?" Luke wondered about the slogan the Spartak fans, which consisted entirely of males, continuously yelled.

Jean Paul nodded "I read in my book that the Spartak team, which took their name from the rebel roman slave and athlete Spartacus, are traditionally known as 'The Meat' because they used to be owned by some meat factory or something. So their fans often sing 'Who are we' to which they respond 'Meats *by ste*' – 'We're the Meat'.

"That is awesome; I like it, what is it again 'Meats buy stay?'" Luke asked. "Yeah close enough" Jean Paul said smiling as his friend. They started singing along and joining in with the Spartak fans much to their neighbours delight. The match ended 2-0 to Spartak. A significant victory over their bitter rivals Dynamo. Both goals were scored by the be-dreadlocked Brazilian teenage sensation Lahinda Anseo.

The increasingly prosperous Eastern European leagues had in recent years become flooded with Brazilian players much like the Western European leagues. The top talents made it but other less fortunate players often became club-less and stranded in a faraway country forced to make a living doing odd jobs until they could make enough money to travel home. Lahinda Anseo would not have pursue such a path; the top European clubs had been attracted by his recent displays and he would be assured of a big money move to one of them as soon as the Russian season finished.

Thoroughly exhausted after the intense and exciting match, coupled with all they had done that day, they decided that even though it was Saturday night they would go back to the hotel straight after the match. They travelled back on the green line until they reached Okhotny Ryad. From there they got the red line to Kropotkinskaya metro stop. Making their way through the labyrinth of lanes and roads until they eventually made it back to Hotel Europa.

"What a day, what city man!" Luke said. "Yeah I cannot believe we did so much in only one day and we still have tomorrow to do more stuff". Jean Paul replied before falling into a deep sleep. The day's activities plus the jet lag all at once taking their toll on him.

Chapter 37

The next day, Sunday, they rose much later than the day before. After eating they made their way over to the Gorky Park area, across the Moscow River. There they did as all tourists do; they wandered around, ate some roasted chestnuts from a vendors stall and did some ice skating. Neither of them were very good at it but it was a quintessential experience for any visitor to Moscow to partake in.

After that they strolled over to the Moscow State University, an immense structure and one of the finest of Stalin's 'Seven Sisters'; seven building ordered by Stalin to be built in the style of the sky scrapers in Manhattan, from there one could truly understand the sheer scale and beauty of Moscow as it has the very best views of the whole city.

That evening back at the Hostel, despite an extremely early start the next morning to catch the train to St. Petersburg to begin the first leg of the Vodka trail, Jean Paul was restless and wanted to go out, particularly as it was their last night in Moscow. They had to be up at 5:30 am the next morning but

Jean Paul wanted to go out to meet people, drink… to really experience Moscow. He was an exceptionally sociable person – always wanting to meet new people. Luke was often amazed by Jean Paul's total lack of apprehension or shyness when it came to socialising with complete strangers he had just introduced himself to in a bar or club. He also had boundless energy; he hated to just sit in and watch TV. As well as all this he was pining to sample some of Russia's finest delicacies – its women.

All this meant that on his last night in Moscow he simply had to go out "I can sleep on the train tomorrow" he said to Luke as he tried to convince Jean Paul that going out was not the wisest thing to do. Luke knew he was fighting a losing battle and conceded that if he wanted to so he should go out but he would need to be back at the hostel at latest by 4:30 am as they had a train to catch at 6:05 am.

Luke was beginning to feel the onset of a cold due to all they had done over the last few days and knew that if he went out he would probably be sick the entire trip. No matter how much Jean Paul called him a '*petit jouer*' for not going out he knew that it was for the best otherwise he might be sick for the whole trip and the whole holiday would be a bust. He figured a good night's sleep and he would be fine in the morning.

Jean Paul asked the receptionist where would be a good place to go out in the centre of town. He decided he would go on a bar crawl. Every place that had been recommended to him by the receptionist he would visit for a *pivo* and Vodka. He left the hostel at 9:00 pm and by 11:30 pm he was arriving at the fourth bar on the list of those recommended to him. He was feeling great, chatting away to tourists and random Russians alike – even though he could not understand much of what they were saying to him. By 12:30 am he arrived at the fifth bar on the list - an Irish bar called The Harp. Jean Paul quickly realised it was an Irish bar in name and theme only; there did not seem to be an Irish person in the place. The staff were certainly Russian. Jean Paul had experienced the same thing back in France and more recently in Spain. 'Irish' on the continent seemed to be a by-word for 'fun' and as such often the best bars in the cities he had lived in or visited were 'Irish' bars – regardless of them actually being owned by Irish people or having English speaking members of staff. He quickly gravitated towards a small group of Dutch tourists who were sitting at the bar.

After an hour of heavy drinking they suggested going to a club they had heard was very good called 'Diamond Lights'. It was not on his list of recommended spots given to him by the receptionist at Hotel Europa but he decided to go anyway. He later discovered why it was not on his list - it was not in the city. It was in the south western suburb of the city. It was a massive place, a three story converted building built during Stalin's reign as leader of the U.S.S.R.

Chapter 38

Wandering from room to room trying to find the Dutch guys he arrived with, Jean Paul glanced at his watch. It was 2:30 am and he was very much feeling the effects of all the alcohol he had consumed over the course of the night. Looking up from his watch he spotted a familiar face drinking alone at the bar. It was the night porter from the hostel. He made his way towards him struggling to hear himself think, let alone be hear over the pumping music. He shouted "Hey man, I know you... from the hostel – I know you, we met you the first night... what is your name again? You showed me and my friend to our rooms. Hi I'm Jean Paul".

He did not receive much of a reaction from Joseph but decided to proceed, as he was pretty drunk by now Jean Paul was more inclined to be insistent and pushy and less prone to be aware of whether his advances were welcome or not. "So... what are you drinking my friend?" Jean Paul shouted in Joseph's ear in order to be heard over the harsh beats of the music in the club. Joseph did not say anything he merely pointed to a bottle behind the bar Jean Paul did not recognise. Nevertheless he could see that is was an indigenous brand of Vodka and from looking at the remaining liquid in the glass in front of Joseph he was drinking it straight and neat.

Joseph had recognised Jean Paul instantly from the moment he stumbled into the bar of the club. He decided to leave him be, his desire to murder was not at its strongest. He was happy, relaxed. He would let his potential victim decide his own fate; if he did not approach him, left him on his own to drink in peace he would leave the little tourist be. But if he disturbed him, came over trying to chat to him then fate would have decided how the night was going to end for both himself and the tourist.

As soon as Jean Paul produced some money a bar girl approached him as he stood beside Joseph who was seated at the bar. He pointed to Joseph glass and mouthed the word 'two' whilst holding up two fingers (as an extra communication tool to indicate what he wanted) – it worked. The ill-advised scantily clad bar girl promptly placed two glasses in front of Jean Paul, filled them one third of the way up with Vodka and without even making eye contact with him plucked the money from his hand and did not return.

Jean Paul was too inebriated and jovial to worry that the stubby Goth had just helped herself to a €3 tip for her services. 'Cheers, my friend' Jean Paul shouted at Joseph as they clinked their glasses together.

As Jean Paul spoke, Joseph was playing out macabre fantasies of how he would make Jean Paul victim #63, how he would do it, his pleasure of marking off another x on his father's chessboard, how it would look with only one square left to fill, only one step from completing his goal. He would occasionally nod encouragingly as Jean Paul spoke so as not to lose his attention.

After three shots of Vodka each Jean Paul looked at his watch. His blurry eyes could just about make out it was 3:25 am. "I should be getting back to the hostel" he shouted in Joseph's ear, as he lent back in his chair, surveyed the room as to which way he needed to take to successfully navigate his way to the exit door of the club. Joseph knew he needed to keep hold of his prey which was imminently about to get away. Earlier in the night he was nonplussed as to whether or not he would kill tonight or not, now the desire was upon him and he would need to act smoothly if he was to achieve his desires. "Why you going so early my friend?" This was the first time Joseph had referred to Jean Paul as a friend – even in his ossified state the word made Jean Paul suddenly well with happiness, he felt accepted. "I catch a train to St. Petersburg at 6:05 am. I check out tomorrow morning. I need to be back at the hostel by 4:30 am. My friend Luke is waiting for me. He is sick so did not come out tonight with me". Despite his drunken state Jean Paul was conscious that Joseph did not have a very strong level of English. As such he tried to speak slowly when he spoke to him and made sure not to use the slang he normally would use when speaking to Luke or the rest of his friends back in Granada. "Ok my friend, very good, I will get you taxi". "Really?! whoa thanks!"

Outside as they waited for a taxi Joseph turned to Jean Paul and said "You know my friend is only 3:30 am now, you still have hour before you need to back to see your friend" – having picked up some English over during his many years of working at The Europa Hotel.

- "Yeah that is true…"
- "How about one more drink?" Joseph said as he revealed an unopened bottle of Vodka from his right inside jacket pocket. Jean Paul's eyes lit up at the sight before him.
- "I probably should get home, though I would love to…"
- "Just one drink my friend, I bring you to a place very special to me, place where no tourists go, you will see real part of Moscow".

The thought intrigued Jean Paul and Joseph could see it.
- "I pay for taxi and I will drop you back to Hotel Europa…"
-"Eh, I probably shouldn't … but what the hell… just one drink yes?"
- "Yes my friend".
- "And you will bring me back to the hostel by 4:30 am?"
- "Yes!"
- "Then let's go" Jean Paul said.

In the taxi Joseph told the taxi driver where they were going, Jean Paul did not understand a thing but decided not to concern himself with such details at such a late hour of the night. After a few minutes driving in the taxi Jean Paul could see that they were going even further away from the city centre and

started to get a little anxious.
- "Hey so where are we going? You know I have to be back at Hostel Europa by 4:30 am right?"
- "My friend, do not worry, we not going far. Another five minutes and we will be there. I have you back in plenty of time". Joseph reassured Jean Paul.

Not wanting to ruin the mood he decided to go with the flow and take Joseph at his word. When the taxi eventually stopped, a few minutes later, Jean Paul could see that the area Joseph had brought him to was fairly run down. Joseph sensed Jean Paul's apprehension at his new surroundings and as the taxi shuffled away into the night, he said "See my friend, the real Russia!". Despite such a throw away comment Joseph's words relaxed him again. "So how come up brought me here?" Jean Paul asked. "This place very special to me, this Bittsa Park. My dog, Dragan, great dog, buried here, I try come here often, pay my respects to him and say hello. Frequently those times are night like this; night when I have drunk little too much and I start to get nostalgic for him".

"Oh, ok, that's cool!" Jean Paul said as they strolled through the heavy forestation of the park, after having successfully negotiated its parameter fence. Jean Paul followed behind Joseph who, he felt, seemed to know every inch of the park.

As they walked, Joseph could not help but smile to himself. He, like everyone else that lived in Moscow, had heard the police say there would be an increased police presence in the park to combat the scourge of 'The Bittsa Park Maniac'. Extra patrols, surveillance cameras, there was even mention of building a police station in the Park. As yet the police station had not materialised. There were more police patrolling the park, at least more than there had been before, which was none. Two police men were now stationed at the front gate of the park. 'What bad guy ever comes in the front door' he thought to himself, allowing a wicked grin to form on his lips as he and Jean Paul continued through the heavy forestation of the park.

The police had erected some cameras in the park, as they had promised the public they would in the press but a homeless drunk, that lived in the park, who had the misfortune to come across

Joseph had told him whilst sharing a bottle of vodka, that most of the cameras were not even real – mere shell cases of surveillance cameras erected (with no actual camera inside) to seem as if the police were watching the area. The attestations of the police had been nothing more than a public relations exercise Joseph felt; half measures to appear to be doing something in order to appease the press and in turn the public. Joseph had quite easily figured out ways of coming and going in the park without the slightest possibility of ever being seen.

Upon exiting the forest, before them was an open flat oval area of grass - ideal for a football match Jean Paul thought to himself. To their immediate right, not twenty paces away, was a solitary tree on a mound. The mound seemed like a concussion on the otherwise pool table like surface.

Joseph made his way towards the area and Jean Paul dutifully followed him "this is place my friend" he said as he sat down at the base of the tree on the mound. As he spoke he withdrew the bottle of Vodka from his inside jacket pocket, opened it, took a mouthful and passed it to Jean Paul. "This is where my great dog Dragan buried". "Really?" was all Jean Paul could muster after taking a mouthful of Vodka from the bottle.

As they drank they spoke about Joseph's dog, Europa Hotel, the Vodka Trail, why they were going on it, where they were coming from, what they did in Spain and of Luke. "Luke is a great guy, it is a real shame he is not here now, you would really like him!" Jean Paul said.

Bottle half drunk, coupled with what he had previously drunk and out in the open air, Jean Paul was now very drunk... and very talkative. It was 3:55 am. "You know" Jean Paul said turning to Joseph "Luke's dad works for the Moscow police force".
- "but is American, yes?" Joseph queried.
- "Yes but his dad speaks some Russian apparently so he manages to get by. In America he was a great cop, Luke told me once when he was very drunk. He never speaks of his dad, they do not get along. Despite now even being in the same city as him he still has not tried to contact him. They have not spoken in years. Don't say anything about this to him though!

"An American cop in Moscow" Joseph said aloud to himself "very interesting" Jean Paul did not really understand what he meant by such a remark. He merely nodded at its validity, shrugged and took another swig of Vodka. It was at this moment Joseph knew who would be number #64 – his masterpiece. Luke would be a fitting and worthy final x on the chess board; son of an American cop working in Moscow it would be perfect. A true master stroke, the greatest serial killer in Russian history, truly a god amongst insects. As he fantasised, Jean Paul chatted and drank and chatted.

"My friend" Joseph interjected and interrupted Jean Paul's ramblings "it is now 4:10 am" he told the tourist who had by now completely lost track of time "we should go now if we are to get you back to the Europa Hotel by 4:30 am". Joseph said as he took the bottle from Jean Paul's right hand, stood up, had a drink and walked behind he unknowing prey who was still seated by the mound near the tree gazing out at the open park in front of him.

"Yeah I suppose you are right" Jean Paul said as he began to muster all his strength and concentration to successfully stand up without falling down again.

As he began to rise, his back was facing Joseph who stood behind him, with his arm cocked waiting for Jean Paul to move into the perfect position. When his ideal target was in sight he struck Jean Paul on the back of the head with all his might with the very vodka bottle they had been drinking from. Jean Paul's body collapsed to the ground in front of Joseph with a sickening thud already blood oozing from his newly acquired wound. Joseph was pretty confident that the tourist was dead but just for good measure he knelt down beside the wound that he had created on Jean Paul's head and proceeded to furiously bash the bottle of Vodka against it until he had managed to completely obliterate the left hand side of Jean Paul's skull. There was now no debate #63 had successfully been killed. The moment of joy of inscribing the x on his hated fathers old chess board would now not be far away and with only one naked square left the moment would be particularly sweet.

He shook himself back to Bittsa Park; he had momentarily teleported himself to his apartment, seated at his small table facing a board with sixty three red x's on it. Looking down at his latest victim he felt nothing but as he was so close to achieving his goal he decided he would send a message to the police.

He opened up his jacket and took his hammer and some one inch nails from his inside left pocket, turning Jean Paul on his back he opened up his jacket and ripped open the shirt the French man was wearing, he straddled Jean Paul's waist and began to hammer nails into the torso of the fresh cadaver.

Some minutes later he had finished. He had hammered ten one inch nails one centimetre deep into Jean Paul's torso from the top of his breast bone near his right arm pit diagonally down just above his left hip. He hammered another line of nails which intersected the original, this time moving left diagonally down towards his right hip.

When he got up and looked down on the pathetic slab of flesh and bone that lay at his feet before him he was pleased with the results before his eyes. An x of nails hammered into Jean Paul's crest, with blood and water oozing from the wounds, the nails were stained red. It looked at if he had just branded his latest victim with a red x and that was exactly Joseph's intention. He left the scene content and still eagerly anticipating getting back to his apartment to perform the ritual on the chess board.

Chapter 39

Luke had been up since 4:00 am waiting for Jean Paul to return. Four and a half hours later the train to St. Petersburg – the first leg of their trip, the train that they were meant to be on at 6:05am had long since departed and there was still no sign of his friend and roommate Jean Paul. Luke was both furious that Jean Paul had gone out at all and increasingly nervous that something bad had happened to his friend. "Why did he have to go out at all?" he rhetorically spat aloud in the empty hostel room.

Luke was sure he would turn up any minute now full of apologies, saying he had got lucky with a beautiful Russian girl. At least he hoped that's what would happen. As angry as he was he was equally sick with worry that something had happened his friend in a strange city where he had no one to turn to.

As the minutes turned into hours his anxiety grew palpable. By mid-day he had already asked the staff at the hostel whether they had seen his friend but they were little help. He had done a quick tour of the surrounding area. He must have rang Jean Paul's mobile phone a thousand times but no one ever picked up.

He had even considered calling his estranged father but instantly dismissed it. By 6:00 pm that day the idea was not so easy to discount. He rang his grandparents after managing to force some food into him in a café in the area. They told him to call his father who was, after all, a police man in the Muscovite police force. If anyone could help he could, they told him.

He could not bring himself to make the call so his grandmother said she would call his dad for him, tell him about the situation; that he was in Moscow, his friend was missing and that he was staying in the Europa Hotel (he had to arrange to stay an extra night when Jean Paul had failed to show up and check out as they were originally meant to that morning). Luke gave his grandparents the number of the hostel and said that he would be back there in ten minutes time and he would wait by the phone for them to call.

As he arrived back at the hostel the phone on the wall in the foyer was ringing, he raced over to it just as the night porter was making his way over to

pick it up. "Hello" he said down the phone slightly out of breath. "Your father will be there in twenty minutes sweetie". Although he was initially relieved that it had in fact been his grandparents on the line and that his father was coming to collect him. His disdain for the man prevented him from saying anything.
- "We love you Luke, give your father a chance - he loves you so much".
Again silence.
- "Ring us again tomorrow and tell us how things are going ok?"
- "Ok, I love you guys too, I better go pack, Goodnight".
- "Night dear".

Luke hung up the phone and headed for his room. "Your family?" queried the same night porter who had shown he and Jean Paul to their room the first night they arrived in Moscow. Joseph was seated at the reception desk. One solitary desk lamp was the only light in the entire room; after ten it was lights out in the common area. It was a way of discouraging guests to frequent the area drinking, talking, playing games and generally making noise all night. "What?" Luke said – he was in another world and had not expected anyone to speak to him.

- "Your family, yes?"
- "My grandparents yeah".
- "Where is your friend tonight?".
- "I do not know", Luke said despondently, "he went out last night and never came back. He might be missing or lost or something…"
- "That very bad news, have you phoned police?"
- "No, not yet… but my dad works for the Moscow police force, he is coming here to collect me soon…I am to go stay with him for a while".
- "He works as cop in Moscow? Is he Russian?"
- "No American… it's a long story".
- "Ok, do not worry about it my friend".
- "Oh, well I gotta go pack cause he will be here very soon".
- "Ok, I will tell you as soon he arrive".

Chapter 40

Jack Wolfe raced through the city streets of Moscow like a mad man, swerving past cars, changing lanes, beeping at innocent pedestrians with the right of way attempting to cross the road. In the heavy rain his one speed windscreen wiper was fighting a losing battle against the torrents of rain cascading against his windscreen obscuring his vision.

His first time to see Luke in more than eighteen months. He thought he would never see him again; he'd planned on killing himself in Moscow in miserable intoxicating solitude yet he was not to know that one day his son would end up visiting Moscow. He was nervous at the prospect of seeing him. Jack tried to prepare himself for the emotional hardship he would feel from the sure to be frosty reception Luke was guaranteed to give him. The emotional memory was all too vivid; his last memories of Luke were of him ignoring him at Aishling's funeral because he blamed him for his mother's death.

Despite all this, he was still happy that he would see his son again, his son was actually in Moscow, actually in the same city as him, he could not quite believe it, so far away from home in American. He had spoken to Aishling's parents some months ago and they informed him they he was doing well studying in Spain but he had no idea that he was planning on visiting Russia whilst in Europe. Jack only lamented that he would be meeting his son again for the first time in so long under such unfortunate circumstances – the Bittsa Park killer had struck again last night. This time, for the first time, killing a tourist. A French tourist visiting Moscow. From the I.D. in his wallet it was obvious he was Luke's Friend whom he had just spoken to Luke grandmother about. How would he break the news to Luke? He could not think straight. His mind was only filled one thought 'thank god it was not Luke!'

Chapter 41

"This is hilarious!" Chikalito bellowed, holding his hands on his stomach trying to quell the piercing pain in it that came from laughing too much. "What a great feeling, you get to see the misery you have caused to someone close to your victim. You killed his friend mere hours ago and here you are talking to him as if you were one of his best friends... wonderful!".

"Yes" Joseph whispered, with a faint smirk dancing in his lips – "it is pretty funny. Even funnier when you consider that he will be next". "Whoa" Chikalito roared "stop, seriously stop" he coughed out through the laugher "this is just too good".

Just then there was a loud and frenetic banging on the front door. It was Luke's dad. After letting him in Joseph went to fetch Luke. All the while Chikalito stood in the corner grinning like a Cheshire cat. When Luke went to the foyer and saw his dad standing before him, he turned to Joseph "Ok, I am going now, thanks for all your help. If my friend turns up, please tell him where I have gone, here is the address" Luke said as he handed him a small piece of paper with his father's address, which his grandparents had given him over the phone, written on it. "Not a problem my friend, hopefully he turn up soon" Joseph said.

Jack stared at the ground trying not to make eye contact with anyone in case they could somehow see in his eyes the horrific fate which had befallen Luke's friend Jean Paul. Chikalito tried hard to stop himself laughing. With that Luke headed down the stairs to the door, bag in hand and out into the street completely ignoring his estranged father.

Swallowing the pain of being almost tangibly hated by his own flesh and blood even in such difficult circumstances Jack said his goodbye to the night porter and followed after Luke.

After a brief but eerily silent car ride they arrived at Jack's apartment. As they walked in Luke fought the urge to tease his father about what a dump he lived in but pride prevented him from opening his mouth. As he lay his bag down he wanted to confide in his dad how worried he was that something might have happened to his friend Jean Paul, that he might be hurt or in danger but again his pride got the better of him; he had stayed angry and silent for this long he was reluctant to give up those feelings of hate he had towards his father – even in these difficult times.

Jack plucked up all his courage, ready to be hurt again by Luke's frostiness, "You look well". "Well you don't" came the cutting response. Harsh as it was it was also true. Jack was just happy to hear Luke's (in Jacks eyes) mellifluous voice. Besides, the last time Luke had seen his father he was svelte and muscular, now he was gaunt in the face and paunchy everywhere else.

"This is some shit hole you live in" Luke said finally relenting a little. "Yes I know, well I don't need much, just a place to sleep, besides the pay is not exactly great". Jack's heart was a glow with happiness just to be able to have such a meaningless conversation with his son. But he knew that he would have to tell Luke about his friend and he would not be thanked for putting it off any longer. "Luke, could you please sit down for a second" Luke looked at his father quizzically in a way that said 'Why?' and 'Where?' (everywhere was filthy).

Eventually he sat down on the arm of the sofa and looked up at his father, eyes scornfully enquiring what was the matter?

Jack took a deep breath squeezed his eyes shut and began. "Your grandmother told me you travelled here with a friend, your roommate whom you live with in Granada, a French guy, Jean Paul right?" "Yeah that's right, he went out last night, he was meant to come back to the hostel at latest 4:30 am this morning but never came back at all, I just hope nothing happened to him".

"Luke I'm sorry but I have some bad news" Jack said as he grabbed a chair from a table to his left and sat down in front of Luke, face to face. "What is it? It is about Jean Paul, is he hurt? Have you found him? Is he in hospital? Is he ok?". "Luke, son there is no easy way to say this, we found your friend in a park outside the city centre this morning. He was dead. Killed".

Luke's heart sank, He could see his dad's lips moving but he could not make out what he was saying; his mind unable to compute – he was not sure, the last word he remembered hearing was "Dead". He snapped back into life, he shot to his feet, and turned on his father accusatorily, angrily. "No, no way, you're wrong. Jean Paul?, Jean Paul Cigcen?, My friend?, How do you know for certain it is my friend?" "His wallet" Jack retorted sheepishly, voice no louder than a whisper, eyes fixed down at the floor.

Luke stared at him incredulously and suddenly he realised his father was telling the truth, his friend and roommate was actually dead. Killed. He felt nauseous, he had a dull, deep pain in the pit of his stomach. "Killed? Are you sure?" Luke asked, slumping himself into the sofa, head in hands. "Yes, unfortunately so. It was the work of a crazed killer who has terrorised the park where Jean Paul was found. We are trying to figure out how or why he would go to Bittsa Park. We are exploring all the possibilities as to how the killer lured him there. Do you have any idea, any idea at all where he went out to last night? Luke shook his head, "he would have started drinking in and around the area of the hostel but how he ended up in some park miles away I have no idea" Luke signing off with an exaggerated shrug of his shoulders just to accentuate the point that he could not help as much as he wished he could. "Ok, ok well we will check that out" Jack said.

"Sorry but I can't deal with all of this right now, I feel like I'm gonna puke. I need to lie down". "Ok, of course, you're right, take my bed tonight; I will sleep here on the couch". Jack said. Luke looked apprehensively at the slovenly bed peeking out of the room to his right but he had more important things on his mind than to worry whether the sheets were clean or not. "Ok, thanks dad, I will talk to you tomorrow". Luke said as he walked into Jack's room and shut the door. Despite the harrowing circumstances of the situation, the normalcy of Luke's words brought back wonderful nostalgic memories of better times back home in New York before everything had gone horribly wrong.

Chapter 42

The next morning Jack woke his son out of a deep sleep, the stress of the previous day must have drained him totally Jack figured. "I gotta go to work son" he said. Luke grunted as he rubbed his eyes. Gradually the large blurry figure that was leaning over him transformed into his father.
- "Luke I gotta go to work".
- "Yeah… em… ok, what time is it?"
- "9:45 am, try and get some more sleep. It will do you good".

A flash of realisation shot before Luke's eyes, his friend Jean Paul was dead, murdered, maybe if he had have been with him none of this would have happened, he should have gone out with him the other night he thought. For a brief moment it had all seemed like a surreal nightmare. What his son was thinking was etched all over his face. Jack didn't even have to ask, he had seen that look many times before. "No I will not be able to go back to sleep now" Luke said. Jack decided not to push the matter.
- "You have money?" Jack asked.
- "Yeah".
- "Well here is some more just in case".
- "Why would I need money?" Luke

begged.

- "Well there is no food in the place… there never is. I can't cook, your mother (he stopped, he daren't make eye contact with Luke in case his eyes held the same hatred as before) … I don't like any of the food here. I usually eat take out – mostly McDonald's. (Looking down at his gut and patting it with mock pride like a mother in her second trimester) this was not cheap you know".

Luke gave an exaggerated smile. Jack took it as his cue to leave. "Ok well I'm gonna go to work, I will be back around 3:00 pm to check on you". "Do you not want me to come with you? Is there nothing I can do to help?" Luke asked. "There are a couple of leads we are exploring and that is what I will be doing this morning. I will be back later and hopefully you can help then by answering some questions about your friend, but for now the best thing to do is try to get a little rest" his father responded. "Ok I'll see you later then" Luke said.

Despite wanting to spend more time with his son who he had not seen in so long, Jack knew he needed to get to work to try and progress 'the Bittsa Park

Maniac' case as far as possible, as soon as possible. As well as being motivated by trying to catch the killer of his son's friend and potentially the killer of eighteen Moscow natives, Jack was conscious of the grave shift in atmosphere at police headquarters since the latest victim – a French tourist had been found brutally slain in Bittsa Park, most likely by 'the Bittsa Park Maniac'. Jack had never see Usmanov so animated about a case since Jean Paul's body had been discovered; he normally reserved such vitriolic energy for criticising him. Clearly the importance of the case in the eyes of the upper echelons of the police force had increased dramatically since news of the latest killing in Bittsa Park broke. The killing of a French student visiting the city was not good for tourism, the case was now international news and as such the pressure to find 'the Maniac' had heightened a hundred fold since yesterday and everybody at police headquarters were aware of this augmented sense of urgency surrounding the case. Mostovoi and Jack (whenever he was lucid, which was not often) had always been determined to catch the perpetrator of such hennas crimes but now it seemed that there was a collective sense of exigency from all parts of the force to catch the killer that was not fully there before. Jack also had the extra motivation to catch 'the Bittsa Park Maniac' after what had happened back in New York with 'Big Foot'. He was determined not to allow one more of these 'sons of bitches' reap havoc on a city he was in charge of policing. Of course, the problem with such a righteous aim was that until his son Luke walked back into his life yesterday, he was more strongly motivated by a determination to drink himself to death.

When Joseph finished work at 9:00 am consulting the note Luke had given him with his father's address written on it he headed straight for Varonofevsky Peroulok where Jack lived. Since 9:30am he had been observing Jack's building, waiting for any movement. Finally at 9:55 am the front door to the building swung open. It was Luke's dad – the cop. He instinctively ducked and then realised that from Luke's dad's stern gaze at the pavement in front of him he may as well have been invisible. Jack got into his Zhiguli 2107 and sped off towards police precinct.

Ladas were the export version of the same car models being sold under the

Zhiguli brand on the domestic Soviet front since 1970. The factory in Russia which produces the cars is one of the biggest in the world, with over 90 miles of production lines, and is unique in that most of the components for the cars are made in house. It produces nearly one million cars a year. The original Lada was a basic car, lacking in most luxuries expected in cars of its time and was modelled after the Fiat 124. Sales to Italy were forbidden by an agreement between the soviet government and Fiat, to protect Fiat from cheap imports in its home market. The Zhiguili was envisaged as a "people's car" like the VW beetle in Germany.

Jack drove a deluxe version; the Zhiguli 2107, with square headlights, refined interiors and a Mercedes inspired grille.

With Luke's dad gone Joseph approached the building and waited for the door to open again so he could enter. He didn't have to wait long, when it opened he snuck in behind an old lady who waddled out. Inside the door, 'Number 28, floor three' he said aloud to himself looking down at the scrawled note Luke had left him in case anyone at the hostel needed to get in contact with him with news of his friend John Paul. He made his way up the flight of stairs directly in front of him, ignoring the elevator to his right. From the fourth floor he could observe the third floor with ease. He stared at the door of apartment '28' hoping for movement.

This time his wait was far longer, it was not until 11:30 am that the door opened and Luke walked out. Having spent hours pacing around his father's dingy apartment thinking about his friend Jean Paul and what had happened to him he decided he needed some fresh air. Russian TV was doing little to help take his mind off things so he decided to go get something to eat despite not being at all hungry. As soon as Luke entered the lift Joseph sprang into life. He ran down to the third floor, to apartment 28 and placed something underneath the door, scribbled a message on the door of the apartment and raced down the stairs after Luke hoping he had not lost him.

On the ground floor there was no one to be seen so he raced out the door and saw a faint glimpse of Luke turning the corner to his left. When Joseph reached the corner he had Luke in his sights, some twenty five yards away from him. He could relax. He shuffled behind him making sure to keep a good distance so as to not be seen. After he was sure he had got an idea of where Luke was going he hurried across the busy street to the other footpath. Eyes fixed on Luke's every stride. He ran on ahead of Luke on the opposite side of the street until he reached the traffic lights. He planned on crossing over to Luke's side of the street and bumping into him seemingly by coincidence.

As Luke wandered down the street in the direction of the golden arches beckoning him forward some fifty paces ahead he was conscious that the person crossing the road in front of him was staring at him. He was anxious not to make eye contact with the stranger but suddenly he spoke. "My friend, hello Luke my friend". Luke was a little taken aback by this and looked up to see the night porter from the Europa Hotel standing before him.

- "Oh hi, sorry I did not see you there".
- "No problem my friend".
- "You live around here?, What are you up to?" Luke asked feigning interest.
- "No, no my mother live this area, just

up the road (Joseph pointed behind him). I try see her often as possible".
- "Oh, ok cool".
- "So what you up to?" Joseph asked
- "Me? I'm just gonna go somewhere to eat down here. My dad lives just up there (pointing to his right) I'm gonna go to McDonalds just up the road there" he said gesturing in the general direction in front of him exaggeratingly with his nose, his hands now back in his pockets.
- "McDonalds? You want real American food? Must go 'Pal Joey's'. Is American diner just few minutes from McDonalds – is very good!".
- "Yeah?"
- "Yes I take you, I need to get something to eat myself".

    The last thing Luke wanted right now was company but not wanting to be rude he said "Em…Ok…Cool…Let's…go".
- "Great follow me… is only a few minutes away".

    As they walked passed McDonalds Luke gazed in the front window forlornly; fantasising about what might have been – eating in solitude without having to make inane conversation. He decided to just suck it up, it would not be that bad. It would hopefully go quickly and painlessly enough. They turned left after McDonalds and walked down a far sparser street. "Is a little bit hidden" Joseph said as they walked. Luke forced a smile. "So has friend turned up? Has been in touch?" joseph asked. Luke was silent. He was unsure what to say. He did not want to get into the whole thing with a veritable stranger. "Em, no, still no word – hopefully he will turn up soon" he just about managed. "I bet he turns up soon. I bet he turns up Dead!" Joseph said as he stopped walking as if to accentuate the finally of his chilling statement. Mid stride Joseph's comment registered with Luke yet he was sure he had misheard, turning around he started to say "What was that?" but instead he was struck on the head with Joseph's hammer as his attacker screamed "You heard me!" knocking Luke out cold in the deserted laneway Joseph had lead him to. The whole incident happened in a flap of a hummingbirds wings.

Joseph bent down picked up his potential masterpiece and got him to his feet. He removed his own coat and placed it over Luke's head. Joseph placed Luke's left arm around his neck whilst he held his right arm around Luke as he struggled to get him back to his apartment. As he walked Joseph gestured to passers-by, who were giving the pair strange looks, intimating that the person he was having difficulty keeping on his feet was his drunken friend whom he was kindly helping to get home.

Chapter 43

Around 2:30 pm Jack arrived back at his apartment building to see how Luke was getting on and see how he was holding up after hearing the tragic fate which had befallen his friend. As the lift opened on the 3rd floor he was instantly struck by a sense of foreboding in the air. Hurrying his pace towards his door his fears were realised when he was greeted by a graffiti scrawl on his door reading '#64'. The number covered half of the face of the door. Fumbling for his keys he clambered in the door, at his feet was a note. His stomach sank; he knew this was not good.

Ignoring the note and leaving his front door wide open he frantically scurried around the apartment shouting and calling for his son – there was no reply. Crushingly he realised there was no one there. He raced back to the note which still lay on the floor. 'Please no, please not again' was all he could think as he unfolded the crumpled piece of paper. With the note now open his worse fears were realised as he started to read the badly typed epistle.

red pig
your son is very lucky! he will become my

masterpiece, the final x - #64
you should feel honour I give him this great place in history
you guys came close to catching me once near my playground but were too stupid to realise you were in presence of true greatness

For a brief moment gruesome visions of Big Foot's massacre of his beloved Aishling flooded his mind, the blood – everywhere. Now there was the very real possibility that the same thing could happen to Luke, it was almost too much for him to cope with. He started to feel faint, the room spun. But as soon as these emotions washed over him almost paralysing him he dispelled them. Now more than ever he needed to be strong; it was the only way he would have any hope of seeing his beloved son again.

Leaving the door open, note clenched in his left hand he fled the apartment, raced out of the building and into his brown Zhiguli 2107. He was trying his best to release himself form the more than year and a half long comatose state that had left him numb to the world, his mind in a vice, blurring all around him: by-products of the nihilism he had felt to all around him since his wife

Aishling had been killed.

By the time Jack arrived at Lubyanya police headquarters, the steely glare he had as a once respected and revered New York cop had returned. Barging into his trusted partner's office he slammed the note onto Mostovoi's desk. "I need your help! My son, read this. My son has been taken by some psycho". Mostovoi had never seen his partner like this before, this stern, this serious... this worried.

"What Jack, your son has been kidnapped? My god no! Wait, you mean the person or people that took your son left this note under your door? Should we not check it for finger prints?" "Ah, when was the last time you ever actually got fingerprints from a note such as this? Nobody ever leaves fingerprints when they leave a note like this! Just read it" Jack contemptuously fired back at his partner. It was a fair point, those types of things only ever happened in Hollywood movies, not in real life; at least not since he had been a cop, Mostovoi thought. He flung the paperwork he was working on off the desk, banishing all possible distractions. He instructed Jack to close the door and began to calmly yet quickly examine the note Jack had thrust into his world.

As he mumbled extracts from the piece of paper, Jack looked on brow dotted with beads of perspiration. 'Masterpriece…', '#64'. "That was written in red on my door also - #64, in red… it looked like red lip stick…" Mostovoi peered up at Jack, over the note which was fixed close to his face, listened intently, seemingly mulling over every syllable Jack uttered and without saying a word returned to reading the note. Again mumbling aloud. 'Great place in history'. As Jack looked on at his partner, reading suddenly, his expressions changed from one of concern to one of confusion. "What?" asked Jack anxiously.

Mostovoi complied with the reason for his changed demeanour. Reading aloud from the letter, emphasising every word 'you guys came close to catching me once near my playground but where too stupid to realise you were in the presence of true greatness'. "We already arrested this guy?" Mostovoi asked his partner. Jack could only shrug.
- "It seems like he is taunting us" Mostovoi posited

- "Yes but who? It could be one of 100's of guys".
- "He's very cocky, he has given us many clues", let's try and piece them together and hopefully make some sense out of them.
- "'#64' could that be murders he has committed? Surely not, that is a crazy number!"
- "Yeah it couldn't mean that, it is way too high of a number to signify that".
- "'My playground' what does that mean?" Jack asked his partner, desperate for him to somehow decipher the notes riddles.
- "'In presence of true greatness'" came Mostovoi's response again quoting from the note in a desperate attempt to suddenly comprehend it. Doing little to ease Jack's distress.
- "God this freckin' maniac has my son, my Luke, we need to figure this out now!" Jack barked beginning to panic. Despite once being a brilliant cop Jack was finding it cripplingly difficult to rediscover that person now when he needed to be at his strongest. The alcoholic haze that had blurred all around him since Aishling was killed would not be easily dispelled, no matter how much he longed to metamorphosis back into in the no nonsense, steely Jack of old, it

would take time to get back to even half of his old self. On top of all this, the panic that ravaged every fibre of his being, which steamed from the fear that something terrible could happen to Luke as it had to his beloved wife Aishling was almost too much to bear. As such, he longed for his partner to put him out of his misery and somehow unlock the mysteries of the note as fast as possible.

- "Calm down Jack, we need to think, as hard as it is for you under these circumstances we need to be cops, professional! It is the only chance your son has right now". Mostovoi sternly scolded his partner in order to get his mind back on the job in hand. Would he be any different if it was his son Rafis who have been taken? Probably not, but he did not have time to think about such things now. He needed Jack to stay focused, so together hopefully they could figure out what had happened to Luke and who had taken him.

- "Yes, you're right. I'm sorry. Continue" Jack said.

- "Wait 'my final x'". Mostovoi said animatedly.

- "What?" Jack asked beleagueredly

- "'My final x'" Mostovoi repeated "that guy…"

- "Who?"

- "The French guy, the latest victim in Bittsa Park, your son's friend".
- "Yeah?"
- "What did the killer do to his chest?" Mostovoi asked leadingly. His voice now tinged with excitement at the thoughts of having cracked an element of the puzzle.
- "He destroyed it with nails, hammered over twenty nails into him".
- "Yes and in what configuration where the nails aligned in his chess?"
- "Well... in some kind of, well in... an x".
- "An x, exactly an x!"
- "You are not suggesting?" Jack asked incredulously of his partner
- "It fits!" Mostovoi retorted. 'my final x' he said aloud again quoted from the note. 'I wonder what is the possible significance of an x' Mostovoi wondered aloud to himself.
- "You are not trying to suggest that my son has been taken by the Bittsa Park Maniac?" Jack said aloud rhetorically. In disbelieving state of shock.
- "It seems so Jack". Mostovoi said seeming impelled to hammer the point home.
- "But... but (struggling to comprehend) it is not possible".
- "Why not?"
- "Just... well... oh my god!"

- "We need to treat this as the reality of the situation until proven otherwise Jack. We are clearly dealing with a highly dangerous individual, a psychopath who it seems is possibly claiming to have killed over sixty people, 'the Bittsa Park Maniac' for whom we have been searching so long for, who has terrorised the city for all this time, who is becoming increasingly brazen in his actions – his note, giving us clues, calling us out, taunting us; saying that we have already arrested him once and let him go. We need to deal with this situation as if this is the person who has your son and Jack we need to act fast if he is going to have any chance of survival". Mostovoi signed off chillingly although not intending to worsen Jack's already troubled mind set.
- "But we have only attributed around seventeen murders, maybe eighteen to 'the Bittsa Park Maniac', now suddenly we think he could have somehow committed over four times that? It is not possible!"
- "I hope for all involved Jack that it is not possible and is not in fact the case, but at the moment that is the ominous direction in which this note is pointing us".
- "Ok I will go along with your theory; he says we have already arrested him near

his play ground, which we are now assuming is a reference to Bittsa Park. How many people have we arrested in Bittsa Park or near it in the last year?"
- "At least one hundred Jack"
- "Well let's cut it down a bit", Jack said; starting to feel an element of himself back in his New York cop days returning. "Let's try and find the guys solely germane to this case and this note whilst negating the others. This is not a homeless person or a drunk we are dealing with. The maniac has used them as his prime target over the years. Also it is not a prostitute or even a women for that matter; the savage strength it would take for the killer to smash a victims' head open with a blunt instrument like a Vodka bottle – we are talking about a young man, relatively well built. I do not think we are talking about a minority here either. This guy is Caucasian (Jack said assuredly remembering from back in his days in the New York police force that in the vast majority of these cases, serial killers are white males aged between 25 and 45). That must eliminate a lot of those one hundred or so people".
- "Yes you are right, but we are still talking about nearly twenty people… at least!"
- "Ok well twenty is better than one

hundred. Call down stairs and get them to bring up the case files on people arrested in and around Bittsa Park in the last year. Tell them we are only interested in cases related to white males, ages 25 – 45, well built. No homeless people and no escaped psychiatric patients" Jack said assuredly; feeling that the note now ruled out these avenues that they had previously pursued.

Mostovoi dutifully following Jack's command and called down stairs requesting all files that matched his partner's required criteria. "They will just be a few minutes…" he said to his partner as he started to re-read the note whilst they waited. 'red pig' he said aloud.
- "It is just his sick way of saying that he is going to kill my son. Red – blood ye know?" Jack said dismissively.
- "Yes that would seem like the logical explanation", Mostovoi concurred, although he was not entirely convinced.
- "Or maybe he is referring to me being Irish?" Jack offered rhetorically, remembering back to his days as a rookie cop in New York when his then boss, Lieutenant Tyrone Wallace, often referred to him as 'red' – a common nickname for many Irish in America due to their particular ting of hair colour. Jack's glib comment was lost on

Mostovoi as he was not familiar with the tenuous connection his partner was making to the note.
- "Maybe", Jack continued, "he is even suggesting that after all this is over he is going to come after me… or possibly that I should just go kill myself for failing my son".

Mostovi was taken aback by his partner's comments. There was an awkward pause for what felt like an eternity to Mostovoi. Jack seemed to be off in another world, in a daze of depression and disillusion. Desperate to bring Jack back to the present, to concentrate on the importance of the matter in hand he racked his brain for something, anything to say. He was struck by the sudden crashing of heavy rain drops against the window of his office. Relieved to have something to talk again, something inane that might just get Jack's mind back on track he said "That's right I heard this morning it was going to be more rain again today – worse that last night they reckon".
- "Who, eh… yeah". (Jack listlessly emerged from his morbid daydream to utter). "Wait! What?" He asked suddenly far more alert that before.
- "It is raining pretty hard out there, they

say it will last all night, will be even worse that last night's rain".
- "Last night… last night… oh my god, last night. That son of a bitch! I know who it is!"
- "What?"
- "I know who it is! I know who has my son!"

With that he sprang to his feet and raced to the door. "Let's go" he demanded. "What Jack?" Mostovoi asked struggling to come to terms with what had just happened in the last few seconds. Jack opened the door and ran straight into a young clerk who worked down stairs in the records department. Knocking the young man over, files falling all over the floor, he did not have time to stop and apologise. He continued down the corridor. Mostovoi, dumbfounded at the events that had just taken place helped the young clerk to his feet, picked up all of the files he had brought with him for he and Jack to examine and raced down the corridor after his partner.

Chapter 44

It seemed like the bump on the back of Luke's head woke up before he did for when Luke actually did regain consciousness his recently acquired bump was already screaming for attention like a new born baby. Every fibre of his head and face hurt, even his eyelashes. He had been in numerous fights before in his life and had been hit many times but he had never felt a pain like this.

He could feel something around his neck obstructing his movement but the first thing he noticed when he opened his eyes was that his hands and feet were tied together with thick tape. He was sitting on the floor with his back to the bathroom wall. Around his neck was what Luke could only assume was a torn strip of bed linen. The cloth had been wrapped tightly around his neck and then secured to the wall behind him through a U nail that had been hammered into it. When he moved the back of his head towards the wall he could feel the U nail on the nape of his neck.

In front of him was a bath tub encased in tile which was fitted against the wall opposite him. To his left, the door of the bathroom which opened out into another room. To his right were the sink and the toilet, each competing to be the most heinously smelling inhabitant of the room. Even in this surreal moment of sheer terror Luke was could not help but notice that the tile in the bathroom was 'North Carolina Blue'. The room looked like it had never been cleaned; mould, dirt, grim and water stains everywhere.

Two thoughts raced through his head 'Where the fuck am I?' and 'I am totally fucked!' He started to oscillate between panic and anger. He would veer toward the panic side with thoughts of what his dad had told him about Jean Paul and how he ended up, to anger when he started to remember who he was with when he was hit, who the culprit was and as such who must have put him where he was now, back to panic when he thought about what a psychopath he must actually be, back to anger when he thought of the ridiculous night porter who in a fair fight he knew he could quite comfortably put in a coma had done this to him and killed his friend Jean Paul.

He started to smash his feet, which were tied together, against the bath in front of him in anger calling on Joseph to come and fight him like a man. After fifteen full minutes of this his wish was granted. The door creaked open, Luke sat frozen in time, mid kick against the bath, staring at the door, waiting, now having completely oscillated to the panic side. Joseph stuck his head round the door and peered in at his prey, eyes glaring at Luke like a rabid dog "Boo!" he said. Luke could not help it, he soiled his pants.

Chapter 45

Racing through the busy late afternoon Moscow streets in torrential rain in Jack's clapped out Zhiguli 2107, was no mean feat but Jack was like a man possessed. Even though he could barely see out the front window as the rain was falling faster that his one speed windscreen wiper could move to dispel it, his refused to slow down.

"Where are we going?" Mostovoi asked as he was flung into the side door of the car for the fourth time, files going everywhere as Jack sped past another car. There was no answer. "Jack!" with this stern shout at his partner Mostovoi had finally managed to break the psychotic trance which had engulfed Jack a few minutes ago back at police headquarters when he declared he knew who had taken his son.

"Jack, where are we going?" Mostovoi asked, calmer this time. "I'm sorry, I know who has Luke and probably who the Bittsa Park Maniac is".
- "Who? How do you know?" Mostovoi implored his partner to fill him in.
- "Last night, you reminded me, last night when I went to pick up my son it was

raining really heavily".
- "Yeah, so?"
- When I went to the hostel where my son was staying I put on a waterproof rain coat to avoid getting soaked. I just bought it a few days ago as 'The Great Thaw' is starting. Last night was the first time I needed to wear it. I keep it in the back just in case I need it (he pointed to the back seat by turning his head and directing his nose in its direction, which made Mostovoi uneasy; particularly at the speed he was driving and the fact that the roads where full of traffic).
- "Yeah so?" he managed to say when Jack's eyes were back on the road in front of him again. "How does this have anything to do with the person who has your son?"
- "The night porter in the hostel where my son was staying was the only person to see me in that raincoat, nobody else saw me in it".
- "So?" Mostovoi snarled, growing impatient. He struggled in vain to try and turn around and look into the back seat at the raincoat but Jack's Formula one style driving made it impossible as Mostovoi was being flung around in the passenger seat like he was on a rollercoaster.
- "My Raincoat is red Mostovoi!" (Jack barked, putting his – on this occasion –

obtuse partner out of his misery). The note said 'red pig' which I took to infer some reference to the impending blood that the maniac intends to spill or me being of Irish decent or that I should kill myself for failing to protect my son, but what if he was being more literal than that? 'red pig' referring to me and to the red jacket I was wearing last night when he first saw me. He already has called us fools for having him once and not realising who he was. Maybe he is trying to taunt us and me in particular with this red reference. The night porter worked at the hostel where my son and his French friend were staying. My son has been taken, a note has been left inside my door and a message scribbled on my apartment's door. Jean Paul Cigcen has been found dead in Bittsa Park, not exactly the most attractive place for a tourist to visit, the latest victim of the Bittsa Park Maniac. The night porter was one of only a handful of people that my son and his friend could have both come into contact with in their short time in this city. That all leads me to believe that the Bittsa Park Maniac is the night porter at the hotel where my son was staying and now this bastard has my son!"
- "Ok, let's say I go along with your theory, where are we going now?"

- "The hostel where my son was staying – The Europa Hotel" replied Jack as he beeped and cursed his way through the otherwise static traffic in front of him.
- "The Europa Hotel?" Mostovoi said aloud to himself. He started frenetically looking through the files which by now had been strewn around the car.
- "Yeah, the Europa Hotel? So what?"
- "Jack, we interviewed a guy who worked there a few months ago. We had to let him go due to lack of evidence. We arrested him around the Bittsa Park area" (as he spoke he buzzed through the files in front of him, discarding anything he did not deem relevant on the floor mat in front of him). "I'm looking for his file Jack, we interviewed this guy only a while back, not more than eight months ago. I can't believe we may have had the Bittsa Park Maniac in our midst and we let him go".
- "Where was I during all of this?" Jack demanded quizzically. Which prompted a look from Mostovoi at his partner that said 'Do you really want me to answer that question?'. Knowing full well that he was more than likely drunk on the job or so hung over as to be more of a hindrance than a help to the case, Jack decided to return to matters in hand.
- "You sure you definitely brought it?"

291

Jack asked looking on at his partner doubtingly, remembering that the files had gone everywhere in his rush to get to his car and commence the chase for his sons captor upon fleeing Mostovoi's office.
- "Yes, I asked archives for all the relevant files relating to the Bittsa Park Maniac that matched our criteria in the last year" Mostovoi said as he started to look into the back seat at the files which had been scattered there and all over the car due to Jack's frenetic driving.
- "But they fell all over the place in our rush to get out of police headquarters".
- "Yes Jack, they did, but I made sure to pick every one of them up before I left because I knew that they might prove very important... ah ha!" Mostovoi declared right hand shooting skywards as his head remained buried in files in the back seats, knees on his passenger seat peering into the rear of the car.

As he made his way back to his front passenger seat he asked his partner "Is this the guy Jack? Is this the guy who you saw last night when you picked your son up from the Europa hotel?" One eye on the road as he negotiated the traffic up ahead he looked at the mug shot Mostovoi had in his hand of Joseph.

"Yeah that's the god dam son of a bitch. That's the inbred bastard!".

- "I cannot believe it!" Mostovoi offered, remembering the DNA tests they had conducted on the suspect at the time. Maybe the tests were flawed he wondered to himself, not knowing about the extremely rare genetic makeup of Joseph. "The idea that we had the Bittsa Park Maniac and let him go!" he said aloud to his partner
- "And now he has my son".
- "Wait a minute Jack are you driving to the Europa hotel? That is right across town. It is not even very likely that if this guy, Joseph Darko, (he said consulting the case file still in his hand) has your son that he will be in the Europa Hotel".
- "True Jack conceded. You got his address in that file of yours? What is it? Where does this prick live?"
- "Jack he only lives on Ulista Novy Arbat, we just passed the turn off for it a minute ago".

Without a moment's hesitation Jack pulled a U turn on the busy ulitsa Mokhovaya ring road he had been driving on, causing a massive pile up of cars. Eyes fixed on the road in front of him he made his way towards ulitsa Novy Arbat and to Joseph Darko's apartment. As they sped off Mostovoi could not help wonder what is they were right? What if they were actually looking for a killer that had potentially killer over sixty people as opposed to the eighteen or so people they originally suspected 'the Bittsa Park Maniac' of committed? He dreaded to think what the consequences and repercussions for all concerned would be, if they were right.

Chapter 46

Inside the bathroom, door closed again, Joseph towered over his masterpiece. Luke still seated on the titled bathroom floor, neck fixed to a U nail in the wall behind him, hands and feet bound, shook uncontrollably.

"You are very lucky boy" Joseph said to Luke as he sat down on the edge of the bath dropping a brown canvas tool bag on the floor with a clank as he sat. "Yeah... how you figure? Luke just about managed to respond. Desperately trying and failing to maintain a cool and tough manner despite the parlous situation he found himself in.

"Not only are you the only one of my victims that I kill in this apartment but you are also my sixty fourth". Frozen with fear Luke could not respond. "Yes that is right so far I have killed sixty three people. Your French friend was #63. He spoke a lot, in the end I was very glad to kill him. I wanted shut him up!" "Screw you" Luke said under his breath into his chest in turn raising his head to look at the monster in front of him., All he could see was a blurry figure, as his eyes were filled with tears. Tears for his fallen friend and for himself.

"I kill my own father when I was lot younger that you are now. He was my first victim". Joseph nonchalantly said as he rustled around in the tool bag that lay at his feet. The sound of clanking tools was like an electric shock to Luke's system; he was suddenly alert again to everything, every vile sight, sound and smell in the room as he awoke from his self-pitying malaise which had over taken him moments earlier.

"Every person I kill I mark an x on my father's chess board to signify it. He would never let me play chess with him, he thought I too stupid to play great game. He was wrong I am very good at chess – better than he ever was! On my chess board (Joseph pointed to the closed bathroom door which lead into the other room) there are sixty three x's; one for every person I kill so far. You are very lucky! You will be my sixty fourth victim. The sixty fourth and final square – my masterpiece and as such I kill you very slowly. You will not be quick like most my other victims, I kill you very slowly. You should feel honoured by this. Your dad and rest of those disgusting pigs are so stupid. They are beneath me, you all are, you are all maggots compared to me and as such I take great pleasure in exterminating people like you".

Joseph's hands emerged from the tool bag at his feet. In his right hand was a hammer. In his left a chisel. Placing the chisel on the top of Luke's left foot, he raised the hammer over his head and smashed it down on his target – the chisel head. The blade of the chisel moved clean through Luke foot until sounding against the title floor on the ground underneath. When Luke saw the alien object protruding out of his foot his brain send waves of pain around his body. The agony was so intense he was unable to scream, he was unable to process this type or amount of pain and he passed out.

"Wake the maggot up" Chikalito trumpeted in over Joseph's left shoulder. Hunched in the corner of the room, standing on the edge of the baths rim he goaded and cajoled Joseph to not let his masterpiece off so lightly.

Complying, Joseph reached into his tool bag placed at his right foot and removed a syringe. Lifting Luke's right sleeve up past his elbow he hovered the syringe over Luke's bare unsuspecting arm. "Yes, yes" Chikalito spat through gritted, discoloured teeth behind Joseph. Joseph placed his thumb on top of the extended syringe and carefully dripped its contents up and down Luke's arm.

Almost immediately Luke sprang into life with a hellacious scream. This time he felt every ounce of the pain. Having successfully revived his victim Joseph casually placed the syringe on the floor adjacent to the tool bag.

"What the shit have you put on my arm you sick bastard!? It's burning my skin! Aggh you fuck! It is burning the crap out of me!" Luke yelled at his emotionless attacker. Picking up the hammer again in his right hand, now looking Luke straight in the eye Joseph coolly offered "It's acid". "What?" Luke questioned, not quite able to believe his ears. "Yes acid, I use it about once a week at hostel to clean sceptic tank. Only in work I must dilute it to use it as it very strong, very corrosive. I have used the full strength stuff on your arm so yes can quite image is very painful. Like I said you should be happy am taking so much time in killing you. You are very privileged".

"Priv...ledged?" Luke just about managed to splutter out over the raging pain and the sheer idiocy of what he was hearing. "You are fucking crazy!". "Crazy? Crazy my boy? Far from it. I am a god" Despite the crippled pain pounding every inch of his body, Luke still managed to look at Joseph as if he had just heard the most mind numbingly stupid thing he had ever heard in his life.

Joseph paid him no regard, instead he grabbed the chisel jutting out of Luke's foot and removed it. The action was met with a symphonic cacophony of screams from Luke. Joseph, now face to face with Luke, looked his masterpiece straight in the eye "be aware, this" he said waving the chisel around the room "is sound proof room, all your screams mean nothing. No one will ever hear you. Scream all you want, you are dead man. Take your rightful place along with others on my chess board. Your daddy and his stupid friends were too dumb to realise they were in presence of greatness when they were in my presence. You pay for their ignorance with your life".

Luke was dumbstruck; knowing all possible crying for help was futile. Now sure his victim had come to fully understand the gravity of his plight, Joseph started hacking away at Luke's left foot like it was a piece of marble. Amid screams which reached deafening crescendos and fell to sickeningly eerie silences when Luke no longer had the energy to scream. At these moments the only sound in the room was that of meat, flesh and bone being hacked, pounded and broken. Until finally Joseph had relieved Luke of his left foot.

Upon looking down and seeing his disfigured left leg Luke wept uncontrollably. This brought howls of laughter from Chikalito and a demonic smile to Joseph's face. He kicked the now lifeless foot to one side and rose up from his perched position on the side of the bath, Chisel in his right hand hammer in the other he began to indiscriminately hack, stab, beat and slash at Luke.

Chapter 47

"What number apartment does this son of a bitch live in?" Mostovoi needed no explanation to whom his partner was referring to. He had never seen him so animated, so possessed with rage, so youthful. As long as he had known him he had a manner that bordered on comatose. Now he was very different from all other cases they had worked on together, this time he was in a race against time to rescue his only son from the crazed clutches of seemingly the most notorious serial killer Moscow and maybe Russia had ever witnessed.

"4A Jack" Mostovoi responded reading from Joseph Darko's case file as they turned the corner on to the street where Joseph lived. Slamming on the brakes they stopped just in front of Joseph's building. Mostovoi followed his partner in leaping from the beaten up car, slamming the door behind him. Tokyo Marui Desert Eagle .50 semi-automatic drawn he followed Jack up the two small steps that led to the entrance of the building.

As he joined Jack he could hear him venting his frustration at something.

"What's up?" Mostovoi asked. "What up? This god dam gate is up!" Jack snarled referring to the large iron gate acting like an uncompromising bouncer refusing entrance to the building. He shook the large gates but they did not budge.. Looking into the foyer he could see no movement, no one coming to allow them in, no one leaving to go to the shops, nothing. Completely deserted.

With one final slam on the gate he yelled "To hell with this" withdrew his 357 Magnum, the gun he had always carried, even back in his days as a cop in New York. He never felt comfortable with any other gun and refused to carry another. He unloaded a full round on the lock of the gates. When he had fired all the rounds in his gun not only was it smoking, but the gate was too. One touch of his finger and the gate compliantly opened.

They raced inside and pushed on the button for the elevator, but it was out of order. "Come on, the stairs" summoned Mostovoi. Despite his new found energy the four flights of stairs would still be a challenge given the garbage he had been fuelling his body with for the last few years.

"Ok let's go" he said as he hobbled up the stairs after his partner. When he reached the fourth floor, Jack was exhausted but one look at the now sinister number/letter combination of '4A' and the severity of the situation became apparent again and he was re-invigorated anew and angry as hell.

Chapter 48

Luke, having realised that no matter how docile or compliant he was in this situation his attacker had no intention of going any easier on him, had become overcome by his primal survival instincts. As Joseph hacked at him, despite his neck, hands and legs being impeded in their movement he flailed, kicked and punched at his sadistic attacker with all his might and although Joseph had caused severe damage to his victim; hacked large chunks of flesh and bone off him, stabbing him countless times with the chisel and intermittently, as if for good measure, whacking him on the head with the hammer to the point where blood spurted and oozed from his various wounds, he was now completely disfigured to the point of being virtually unrecognisable to anyone who knew him, he was growing increasingly frustrated by his preys' defiance.

Despite inflicting horrific damage on his victim Joseph was un-used to dealing with such an unruly victim. In the past his victims had been so drunken and confused as to never put up much of a flight but this one was different, even with his movements retarded through strapping he was very strong. As Joseph's frustration grew, Chikalito's grin did also. Perched in the corner of the bathroom like a menacing vulture he found Joseph's difficulties highly amusing.

"Hold still you maggot" "Fuck you, you fucking virgin" Luke growled back at Joseph as he kicked him again with all his might. This only made Joseph even more angry as he started to hit Luke with all the strength he could muster.

Chapter 49

Loading a new round into his gun Jack moved Mostovoi to one side and standing square in front of the door he bashed it open with his right foot. Not bothering to even check whether the area was safe to enter, he leapt into the room, Mostovoi followed after checking it was actually safe to enter – his police training getting the better of him and besides he was on a rescue mission not a suicide mission.

Now inside apartment 4A, they were greeted by a deserted room and a horrendous smell. A single bed in the right hand corner of the room, cooker in the left, table with one chair to their immediate left. "There is no one here!" "Wait" Jack said as he spotted the door to his immediate right, the bathroom he postulated. He again bashed the door in but to his despair again there was nothing but a deserted room before them. The only thing that inhabited the room was a stomach churning smell emanating from the toilet.

"What the hell!? "What the hell Mostovoi?" Jack said turning to his partner dismayed, "you told me this was where this prick lived!". "That… that is what his case file said Jack, that is where he lived when we arrested and interviewed him only a few months ago. Maybe he had moved…?"

Jack was floored, numb, speechless. He started to panic thinking about what could have happened and might be happening to his only son and all the time they had wasted coming to this deserted, disgusting apartment.

Jack started pacing up and down the main room of the apartment, in total dread, struggling to formulate a coherent thought as to what to do next? "It's hopeless, hopeless, my god, my son, he is dead by now, my beautiful son, gone…! No, please, god, no, please, Luke, god, Luke, please". "Jack!" Mostovoi grabbed his partner and physically shook him, "There is still hope. Let's go to Hotel Europa and see if they have a current address for this guy ok Jack? Ok? Let's go! Ok?"

"Yeah, eh, ok, let's go" Jack mumbled coming back to reality. "Thanks!" he said to Mostovoi. He needed that. Mostovoi had always been a good partner and Jack appreciated him now more than ever. In this adverse time he loved him like a brother.

They raced down the stairs again, in the foyer they saw an elderly man, bent down on one knee examining the now destroyed lock on the gate. As they approached him they could see that he worked in the apartment building. "Who did this to my gate? The animals, this city is full of animals, my gate, who did this?"

"We did" said Mostovoi. "Why? What did I ever do to you?" the old man queried angrily, anger instantly turning to fear he signed off "I am sorry, forgive me please do not hurt me". "We will not hurt you. We are the police, not the mafia". "The police" the pint sized man questioned. "Why would you do this?"

"Who are you?" Mostovoi demanded sternly. "My name is Dimi, Dimitar Borinoff. I look after the day to day running of the building for my employer, the woman who owns this building, Lady Karlovic". Happy with the answer he received Mostovoi offered "We were looking for someone and could not open the gate to the building so we forced our way in, do not worry we will pay for the damages". "Who were you looking for?" Dimi asked.

"He is not there" Jack interrupted conscious of the time, urging his partner to hurry this conversation up so they could get going. "Hold on" Mostovoi urged realising that Jack may still be in a daze and not know that this man could potentially help them. We were looking for "Joseph Darko, in apartment 4A but he is not there". "Ah Joseph, he is not in trouble is he? Such a nice young boy, a little shy maybe but always very polite".

"No, no Mostovoi said (not wanted to shatter the elderly man's illusion of Joseph) he is just helping us with an investigation". "4A you said, you will not find him there" Dimi said "It is true he used to live in that apartment for many years but there was a problem in the last few month or so with the plumbing in that apartment so we had to move him to a new one. Smells awful in there now, so it does"

"Where? Where? Does he still live in this building? Jack asked. "Yes, yes, he now lives on the top floor, apartment 7D". Dimi said wondering what all the fuss was about. As soon as Jack heard the new number/letter combination he turned on his heels and raced up the stairs again. This time there was no hobbling gait; he raced up the stairs like it was an Olympic event, one he had devoted all his life to training for.

"Thank you for all your help" Mostovoi called over his shoulder to the elderly man at the gate, who looked slightly bemused at what he had just witnessed, as he raced up the stairs after his partner.

Chapter 50

"I have had enough of this" Joseph screamed with frustration as he flung his hammer and chisel to the side of the room. "You are going to die now, you vermin" he snarled. "Yes! yes! Do it!, Kill this son of a filthy pig!" cackled Chikalito. Reaching down near his tool bag he arose again with the syringe, now half full, of corrosive acid. By passing Luke's flailing arms and legs he moved to the side of #64 and crouched down beside him.

"This is where you die" he said psychotically to Luke as he squeezed a droplet from the syringe onto Luke's cheek, burning into his flesh he refused to give his attacker the pleasure of his screams of pain. All he could think of was his mother and his father – he wanted to remain strong for them. Moving the syringe to Luke's neck, Joseph whispered "let's see you stay quiet with all this shit inside you big man" as he injected the remaining dose of liquid into the neck of his prey. In doing so Joseph stepped back from his masterpiece, sat back on the edge of the bath and allowed a delicious wave of *shadenfeude* wash over him as his pernicious final act.

Chapter 51

Having reached the seventh floor, this time Jack did not need to stop to catch his breath before bashing down the door. With his partner in hot pursuit behind him still making his way up the stairs Jack leapt into apartment 7D. Once he had dealt with its front door. Again the apartment was deserted. Again he was greeted by nothing but silence.

As Joseph squeezed the last droplet of the acid into his latest victim's neck Luck momentarily wailed like a banshee; a sickening last cry for help until he could no longer scream or speak at all as the acid surged forth destroying all it came into contact with inside his trachea. Chikalito laughed himself sick in the corner of the room.

By the time Mostovoi had reached the door of apartment 7A Jack was firing shots into the door of the bathroom to his right, beating the door open he fired several bullets at the demonic figure that was perched over his son, or at least he sensed it was his son – the deformed figure on the bathroom floor had been beaten and hacked to a bloody pulp. Mostovoi leapt into the room.

"No, no it is not meant to end like this" Joseph cried "I need to mark the last x on my chess board". Mostovoi fired a shot at Joseph's shoulder; not to kill him, primarily to incapacitate him and to shut him up. It made little difference, he continued crying out for his chess board. "#64, #64, let me mark it on the board". Jack was desperately trying to untie his boy but momentarily was lost in rage and started to beat Joseph with the hammer he found on the floor of the titled bathroom. "You sick bastard, you son of a bitch, you are dead! You hear me? Dead!" Despite begin whacked repeatedly all Joseph could think of or talk about was square 64, the last x, how beautiful the board will look with all the squares filled in with red x's.

"No Jack, not like this, Jack, you are still a cop, No!" Mostovoi urged pulling Jack off Joseph. "Look after your son Jack, he needs your help". Awakening from the rage that had overcome him "Yes, you're right, my son he said (turned back to Luke on the floor) my beautiful son (desperately trying to unravel the ties which had bound him) Call an ambulance!" he demanded.

"Come with me you sick bastard" Mostovoi said to Joseph as he dragged him out of the bathroom and into the main room.

Luke tried desperately to speak but couldn't, the caustic liquid was rampaging through his system, had destroyed his voice box and vocal cords. His eyes filled with pain from the ordeal he had had to endure and the torture which had befallen him now filled with love for his father, he felt an immense love for him having come to rescue him and yet he felt equal amounts of sorrow for having ignored him for so many years, for blaming him for the death of his mother – all that wasted time and emotion. Tears rolled down his face. He did not have to say a word. His father understood every emotion Luke was feeling as if they were literally etched upon his face. They looked at each other, face to face, inches away from one another. In that moment there was a deep understanding between them – something that had been missing for years, a bond that Jack never thought he would experience with anyone again let alone with his estranged son. His heart broke, it swelled and his stomach sank with unerring and unconditional love for his only son, for the life they used to share together and for the hopelessness and horrendousness of this situation they now found themselves in.

He held his only son in his arms and wept. "I am so sorry, my son, Luke, I am so sorry for everything, it is all my fault Luke, you, your beautiful mother, I have ruined all of our lives – what I would give to take it all back. Go back to when everything was good again between all of us".

Despite the excruciating physical pain he was feeling Luke lifted his head up and looked deep into his father's eyes, as he blinked floods of tears cascaded down his face. It was a look that did not need to be complemented or sullied with words. It said that he forgave him for everything and loved him with all his heart. Mustering his last ounce of strength he arched his neck and kissed his dad on the check and immediately collapsed back in his father's arms. Now lifeless. Now dead. His body could no longer stand the pain.

"No!!" Jack wailed "No, my beautiful... call a god dam ambulance

Mostovoi!" he yelled in desperation into the other room. "I have Jack" came Mostovoi's meek response "they will be here in a few minutes… and so will back-up". With that he gently closed the bathroom door to allow his partner to be alone with his son. He was overcome with emotion. Turning around, he jumped on the now handcuffed Joseph. Straddling his torso he beat him with the butt of his gun. Still all Joseph cared about was the sixty fourth x. "Please, please just let me fill in the last x. Then I will gladly go to jail". "Shut the hell up you sick bastard" Mostovoi squawked bashing in Joseph's bottom front teeth with his gun. It made no difference. The noise of 'the last x', '#64', 'my chessboard', 'the last square' was all that filled the room.

Mostovoi rose up off Joseph in disgust. He spat in his face and went to the hall and willed back-up and the now useless ambulance to hurry the hell up so he could leave this nauseating place and get away from this revolting psychopath who was still jabbering on about '#64' as he lay handcuffed on the floor.

Chapter 52

Reporter Yevgani Stankovic had been sitting at his desk for over an hour and had as yet not typed a single word. All the other journalists had already filed their copy for tomorrow's paper and his deadline was fast approaching. Looking up from his key board he was faced with his editor scowling at him and frantically tapping his watch. The five empty cups of coffee that now occupied his desk had brought little inspiration. Constantly adjusting his glasses, his neckerchief or rubbing his goatee had not helped either. He had no idea where to start.

    Tomorrow was the last day of the most notorious murder trial in modern Russian History. 'The Bittsa Park Maniac' had now been newly dubbed 'The Chess Board Killer'. Claiming to have killed sixty four people, the police had only charged him with fifty one due to a lack of evidence. This was still far more than they had ever suspected 'the Bittsa Park Maniac' of ever committing. There was much consternation and anger as the perfunctory manner in which the case had been dealt with by the police. To the citizens of Moscow it seemed a little too coincidental that mere days after the murder of a French tourist, Jean Paul Cigcen, the murderer was brought to justice, that the police had not done enough when Russian people (homeless drunks and prostitutes or not) were being slain. The concern and annoyance had increased since the number of those killed had been discovered. Some wondered would the killer ever have been caught if he had not started killing non Russians? The trial had been expedited due to the fact that the killer, Joseph Darko, had admitted full culpability for all the murders, showing no compunction for his victims nor any attempt to tergiversate in admitting to his crimes. The only sticking point was that 'The Chess Board Killer' wanted to be charged with more murders; he wanted to be charged with sixty four murders, but the chief investigator on the case, Pavel Mostovoi, who had been promoted since the capture of the killer from detective to rank of lieutenant, could only find evidence of fifty one crimes committed.

It had emerged during the trial that Darko had been hearing voices in recent years, the voice of Russia's most notorious serial killer Vitali Chikalito. Apparently he had been encouraging Darko to kill young boys and girls, to molest and mutilate them – a point Darko has been at pains to say he rejected. Stankovic wondered whether he should exploit the human interest aspect of the story; the American cop, working in Moscow, who lost his only son to 'The Chess Board Killer', who had been his last victim and who had died in his father's arms. He felt the fact that Jack Wolfe, who had since quit the Muscovite police force and whose life had spiralled into a mire of utter depression since what had occurred would be attending the final day of the trial tomorrow as he had all thirty six days of it so far would certainly be a fruitful avenue to pursue.

Then a moment of inspiration, he had it. He feverously started to type away at his keyboard. The sight of which brought delight to his editor's heart. The story that would be front page of tomorrow's Tvoi Dyen began:

Check Mate
Yevgani Stankovic reporting

Chess obsessed psychopathic serial killer, Joseph Darko, dubbed 'The Chess Board Killer' by this very reporter will be sentenced tomorrow. He started his murderous crusade with the aim of being considered the most notorious serial killer in all of Russian History. Only being tried on fifty one murder counts tomorrow compared to Vitali Chikalito's fifty two means that in his macabre battle of chess with his former idol and in later years mentor he has lost.

The Rostov Ripper has taken Darko's queen and this will be the point that will most infuriate him far more than actually being caught. 'The Chess Board Killer' will spend the rest of his days in prison when he is sentenced tomorrow. He will forever consider the police and Chikalito as his nemeses for taking away his coveted crown as Russia's most notorious Serial killer.

Chapter 53

Throughout the last day of the trial and even up to when the judge was about to hand down his sentence, Mostovoi noticed that his good friend and former partner was nowhere to be seen. "Maybe it is all just too much for him to cope with" he said aloud to himself as he took his seat in the bustling court room. Journalists crowded the public gallery, filming everything, clambering for the best possible position to take photos.

Luke's grandparents had wanted to come to Russia to support Jack, but the burden was too great for them to bear considering their age and fragile state, the trip alone from North Carolina to Moscow would have been a significant undertaking. Luke's friends back in America, Jean Paul's friends and family in France as well as their friends back in Granada, along with Luke's girlfriend Laura, were all huddled around various television screens wherever they were to hear Luke's killer being brought to justice.

As the judge took his seat it required repeated slamming of his gavel to get order in the court. Eventually when everybody had calmed down he requested that the defendant be brought in.

As Joseph Darko entered the court room from the side entrance, wrists and ankles shackled, flanked by four armed guards either side of him, there was pandemonium in the courtroom; relatives of some of Joseph's victims hurled abuse at him, journalists and photographers hustled and harried to get the best shot – that one shot of 'The Chess Board Killer' that would be seen all around the world.

"Order, Order, Order in my court" judge Bogdanovic yelled "I realise that this is a unique and difficult situation for some people in court today but if you cannot control yourselves I will hold you all in contempt of court". Eventually everyone took their seats again and order was restored.

There was an iron four by four foot cage that had been erected especially for this trail in the middle of the courtroom. This was where Joseph spent the last thirty six days of the trail. Inside was a solitary stool for him to sit on, if he became tired of standing.

Entering the cage for one last time Joseph was positioned directly in front of judge with the defence and prosecution teams on either side of him. Behind the cage were the public galleries.

It had been erected for the defendant's protection more than anything else, in case a riot broke out and family members of Joseph's former victims decided to exact their own form of retribution for their loved one's deaths. Despite its original purpose it actually had the effect of making it seem like the police were locking up a wild animal unable to control its primal urges. The cage made it seem like there was impending danger in the air whenever Joseph was in the room even with all the guards that occupied the courtroom. It was like manna from heaven for the attending journalists though. It only added to 'The Chess Board Killers' mystic and made for devilishly enticing copy.

"Joseph Darko I will now sentence you for the crimes you freely admit to having committed" The judge proceeded to painstakingly go through every crime the police had sufficient evidence to convict Joseph on – all fifty one of them – until finally he said "for the crime of killing Jean Paul Cigcen the court finds you guilty and lastly for the crime of kidnapping, torturing and killing Luke Callagahan the court finds you guilty as charged. As the state has passed a moratorium on the death penalty I cannot sentence you to death for your heinous crimes as much as I would like to. Instead you will serve a life sentence of thirty years for all fifty one of your victims. You will serve a total of one thousand five hundred and thirty years in jails for the crimes you have committed. Joseph Darko you will die in Jail for your crimes, you will never get the benefit of an early release and in many ways that might be a more fitting punishment for you. It is your right at this time to address the court if you wish".

When Joseph Darko began to speak a pin could be heard dropping in the court room. It seemed that even the judge who had handed down the sentence was mesmerised that a man who had been capable of committing such evil crimes. "I ask only this of the court, that I be allowed to mark the last x on my chessboard – that which signifies the murder of my 64th victim, Luke Callaghan, that I be allowed to complete my masterpiece. As well as this I request that I be tried for all sixty four murders which I committed and have admitted to carrying out. I have killed many more that fifty one people. Please keep looking for evidence of this and when you do find it feel free to charge me with them. I do not regret my actions, if I was still free I would continue to kill; sixty four was my goal but I know I would never have stopped. I need to kill like you need air to breath. Human life is worthless and meaningless to me. I am a god and you are all mere maggots compared to me. You all deserve to be put into a meat grinder and eradicated. You are all no more valuable than pork meat. The real crime is to live like you do. Life turns away from those like you. Then life sends those like me to you. I was a father to all those I killed. I gave birth to them - birth into a new world, the next world. I marked every one of their deaths with the sign of Christ on my chess board- with an x. Saint Nicholas is our Patron Saint and he is also the patron Saint of Greece. In Greek x is the symbol of Christ. The police should take no credit for catching me, I burned myself; I led them to me – they are nothing more than worthless pigs. I think in a way I wanted to get caught. If I had never been caught how else would I receive acknowledgement and notoriety for my achievements; for being the most notorious serial killer in Russian History?".

"Is that all?" the dumbfounded judge just about managed to stutter. Nearly everyone in the courtroom had been left open mouthed and in frightened awe of Joseph's ghastly soliloquy.

Fixing his glare on the judge as intensely as any perfected by the masters of Russians chess when scrutinising the board before their next move he said "Yes that is all I have to say, remember I am Russia's most notorious serial killer having killed sixty four people so please keep looking for the rest of my victims". It was as if Joseph's speech had left the court in suspended animation for several moments and it was only now that they were processing Joseph's comments that the place ebulliently erupted into an all-out riot.

"Remove him for the court" the judge yelled and Joseph's cage was opened for him to be led away. He walked out of the court as calm as a Hindu cow - as if he was strolling along a beach on a summers day; without a care in the world. This sight only made the family members in the court baying for his blood all the more angry.

Just as Joseph was approaching the door to exit the court and commence his sentence screams of panic could be heard. A large elderly man rose from his seat at the front of the court, in his right hand, a gun. He fired a single round hitting Joseph in the chest. "Die you bastard, Die!" the old man yelled in English in an accent that was all too familiar to Mostovoi. His words were like a bullet piercing his soul. Without hesitation the four guards, which were flanking Joseph unleashed their guns on the stocky old man, spraying him with a volley of bullets.

"Clear the court" the judge cried, as paramedics rushed in and removed the defendant from the court to treat his wounds. Family members and journalists were herded out of the court. Mostovoi raced to the fallen man. As he approached his heart sank. His worst fears had been realised.

"Jack, …no", the 'elderly man' was in fact his former partner Jack Wolfe. Without the hat he had been wearing, it was painfully obvious that in fact his old partner had been in court the entire time. He had dressed up as an elderly man, hunched over, wearing a shabby trench coat, glasses and aided by a walking stick. Mostovoi never for one moment suspected it might have been Jack.

Mostovoi had not spoken to him since the trial commenced. No matter how hard he tried the increasingly introverted Jack shunned all contact. As he got closer to the body, blood oozing from a multitude of cavities it was heart wrenchingly evident that his former partner was dead. Bending down over him he said "Why Jack? but as soon as the words passed through his lips he realised how inane they were; he knew very well why Jack had taken justice into his own hands. Who was he to question a man who had, years ago, endured his wife being massacred by a serial killer only to have the same fate befall his only son? Who was he to judge? "Until you have walked a mile in another man's shoes…" he said aloud to himself as he closed over Jack's eyes and covered his head with his jacket.

Turning to the guards, who had only been carrying out their jobs as they had been trained to do, he said "this is a great man, a great muscovite policeman has died today". Bemused and a little confused the guards saluted Mostovoi and exited the courtroom leaving him to be alone with his former partner one last time.

Prologue

"They did not even execute you?! That shows how little a danger you are considered" the shadowy figure taunted Joseph from the corner of his six by six foot cell. "They wanted to, but they have put a moratorium on executions. They don't do that anymore" came Joseph's impassioned response trying to defend himself. "If you were dangerous enough they would have killed you. Sure they only charged you with fifty one murders. That is less than me. I am still Russia's most notorious serial killer. You are only second and second is nothing. You are pathetic".

"Listen to me you sick child molesting impotent freak, I killed sixty four people, thirteen more that you. You are nothing compared to me Chikalito". Joseph said. Unperturbed Chikalito barked back through his disgusting yellow teeth "According to the rest of the world I am Russia's greatest serial killer". "Oh yeah?, Well listen to this then you annoying bastard" Joseph said as he rose to his feet. His former idol had now become his hated nemesis, anathema to him - a festering boil that irritating every nerve in his body. He was desperate to get one up on him.

Rising up and summoning the guard who was a constant sentinel outside his door. He spoke through the letter box hatch "Tell the police that in my old apartment building, where I used to live, down in the basement, there is a storage area with individual small storage units for each of the inhabitants of the apartment building, I am the only one who really uses one. My unit is marked 4A. In that storage unit is a man. A former manager of a supermarket I used to work for many years ago called Vadim Gudhov. I have been keeping that asshole alive in that that three by three foot storage unit for the past ten years. Starving him for days on end then feeding him only dog food. He killed my dog Dragan many years ago and I have been making him pay ever since. I cut his tongue out a long time ago. According to my calculations he has not had anything to eat or drink in over sixty days. He is certainly dead by now because I have kept him very weak and feeble – living on the edge of life and death for many years. Go and tell your friends that he is number sixty five that I have killed and at very least by their pitiful calculations it makes me level with that disgusting insect Chikalito who killed fifty two people".

Dumbstruck the guard ran to tell the chief guard what Joseph had just told him. Satisfied that the police would eventually find Mr Gudhov's dead body in the basement of his building he turned around and glared at Chikalito, who was speechless, "See?! I am number one and do not ever forget it! Check mate!"

The End.

Printed in Poland
by Amazon Fulfillment
Poland Sp. z o.o., Wrocław